Stories by Contemporary Writers from Shanghai

GAME POINT

T0095722

This book is edited and designed by the Editorial Committee of *Cultural China* series

Text by Xiao Bai
Translation by Wu Xiaozhen
Cover Image by Quanjing
Interior Design by Xue Wenqing
Cover Design by Wang Wei

Editor: Wu Yuezhou
Editorial Director: Zhang Yicong

Senior Consultants: Sun Yong, Wu Ying, Yang Xinci
Managing Director and Publisher: Wang Youbu

ISBN: 978-1-60220-246-7

Address any comments about *Game Point* to:

Better Link Press
99 Park Ave
New York, NY 10016
USA

or

Shanghai Press and Publishing Development Company
F 7 Donghu Road, Shanghai, China (200031)
Email: comments_betterlinkpress@hotmail.com

Printed in China by Shanghai Donnelley Printing Co., Ltd.

1   3   5   7   9   10   8   6   4   2

GAME POINT

By Xiao Bai

Better Link Press

Foreword

This collection of books for English readers consists of short stories and novellas published by writers based in Shanghai. Apart from a few who are immigrants to Shanghai, most of them were born in the city, from the latter part of the 1940s to the 1980s. Some of them had their works published in the late 1970s and the early 1980s; some gained recognition only in the 21st century. The older among them were the focus of the "To the Mountains and Villages" campaign in their youth, and as a result, lived and worked in the villages. The difficult paths of their lives had given them unique experiences and perspectives prior to their eventual return to Shanghai. They took up creative writing for different reasons but all share a creative urge and a love for writing. By profession, some of them are college professors, some literary editors, some directors of literary institutions, some freelance writers and some professional writers. From the individual styles of the authors and the art of their writings, readers can easily detect traces of the authors' own experiences in life, their interests, as well as their aesthetic values. Most of the works in this collection are still written in the realistic style that represents, in a painstakingly fashioned fictional world, the changes of the times in urban and rural life. Having grown up in a more open era, the younger writers have been spared the hardships experienced by their predecessors, and therefore seek greater freedom in their writing. Whatever category of writers they belong to, all of them have gained their rightful places in Chinese literary circles over the last forty years. Shanghai writers tend to favor urban narratives more than other genres of writing. Most of the works in this collection can be characterized as urban literature with Shanghai characteristics, but there are also exceptions.

Called the "Paris of the East", Shanghai was already an international metropolis in the 1920s and 30s. Being the center of China's economy, culture and literature at the time, it housed a majority of writers of importance in the history of modern Chinese literature. The list includes Lu Xun, Guo Moruo, Mao Dun and Ba Jin, who had all written and published prolifically in Shanghai. Now, with Shanghai re-emerging as a globalized metropolis, the Shanghai writers who have appeared on the literary scene in the last forty years all face new challenges and literary quests of the times. I am confident that some of the older writers will produce new masterpieces. As for the fledging new generation of writers, we naturally expect them to go far in their long writing careers ahead of them. In due course, we will also introduce those writers who did not make it into this collection.

Wang Jiren
Series Editor

...
in you I see dirty
in you I count stars
in you I feel so pretty
in you I taste god
in you I feel so hungry
in you I crash cars
...

—*Ava Adore* by Smashing Pumpkins

I

Those of us who hung out together never made any fuss. I mean, nobody would gawk when someone resurfaced after a few weeks or months. Or no one would act surprised if whoever was at a dinner party or not. Indeed, you couldn't tell the whereabouts of the people in our gang unless you counted who was at a dinner party. However, nobody would ask why. You couldn't pry like an idiot. Otherwise, congratulations, you'd soon become the clown that nobody would talk business with. Yes, business, literally.

If a guy who had been at a dinner party every night except tonight, you'd better pretend he had never been here. If you were asked why this guy didn't show up, you'd better make something up off the top of your head. Like, well, I heard the other night that he was going to Thailand. Or, he's seeing a college chick from Xinjiang. She's got beautiful blue eyes. Just like those Soviet Union prostitutes working at Hotel Equatorial. Oh yes, it was years after the collapse of the former Soviet Union, yet we were still not used to the term Russia. In fact, people at a dinner party would spin all sorts of story about who is where, and the most imaginative would follow through down to details such as the sexual particularities of the guy in question. Nevertheless, nobody would take any story seriously.

I hadn't seen Lobster for a while. More often than not, others believed that I knew what he was up to. In their eyes, Lobster, Lü Yan, and I should know each other's whereabouts, since the three of us rented an apartment together near the Yandang Mansion.

The other day when I asked Lü Yan where Lobster was, he said Fuzhou. Tonight at dinner, he said Wuhan when someone else asked him.

I felt drowsy in Lü Yan's car. Eleven in the late evening was the drowsiest time of the day. After midnight I would be wide awake. Lü Yan was garrulous after a couple of drinks. His voice stretched out thin and far like a broken string drifting in the wind. I was a bit bored. It felt comfortable inside the car when there was heavy rain outside, a feeling that must keep before everything. I slouched further as the car glided dreamily ahead. The rain had something to do with you, or nothing. By an extension of this logic, this city also had something to do with you, but you must think hard before you knew what that something was. Such a sense of distance made you feel light.

The rain abated. I let the car window down a bit. The air felt wet and cool. Lü Yan was talking to me, but I wasn't listening. Sisi was humming in the back seat. These days she was Lü Yan's girl. The car slowed down when it turned from Fumin Road to Changle Road, where at night it became a de facto garage, with vehicles of all sizes parked in whatever space available. I catch Lü Yan saying, "Lobster has his eyes on money-making opportunities." I laughed. It was no surprise at all. Lobster was always looking for ways to make money. Last year when we rented an office from the Chinese Academy of Sciences, he had millions sitting in his bank account, but he was still busy hustling for more.

"Wanna go for a drink at the Jinjiang Tower?" Lü Yan was raised in Beijing. His grandfather was a senior military officer. His parents worked for a military institute. So he looked like a Beijing native; tall, big, with a pale square face and a puckered mouth. I guess he was never hungry when growing up. After all, military families were privileged. I was tall too, but by no means big. Poor nutrition at childhood shows. Lü Yan could go bar hopping, but I couldn't. Again, that was related to the god damned nutrition. People of my generation turned out strong or not depending on what our parents were. It had not much to do with whether there was money or an influential official in the family, but a lot to do with what our parents were. A friend of mine was strong because his dad was a cop at a prison farm in Anhui Province, where they fished daily at the local reservoir and ate hare every so often. Another friend of mine was strong because his mother was the head of a nursery, where there was plenty of milk to spare.

I told him to drop me off at Yandang Road and have fun on his own. Lü Yan grumbled. Idiotic women like Sisi could never party enough. She made a clamor. I advised her with a straight face, "It's no fun drinking out on such a rainy night. A party of two in bed is much better."

Lü Yan said he had no energy for any bed party. He spoke Shanghai dialect with a Beijing accent. I said she could lead. Sisi giggled.

"He hasn't been to dinner for a while. I asked about and found he was in hospital. Proctitis operation. We visited him in the hospital. He said he had gone through the procedure several times. He even turned over to show Lobster his asshole. Fuck, can any asshole look pretty? He asked for Lobster's opinion on the incision. Do you know how Lobster replied?"

I looked blankly out of the car window, not sure who he was talking about.

"He replied, 'Three nice cuts. Your butt now looks like a Mercedes Benz.'"

The rain seemed to have stopped. It cleared up, dark and shining like memory. I like crisscrossing the city at this time of the day, especially in this time of the year. It might be warm during the day, but it was cool at night, or I would say a bit too cold for me to be just wearing a linen jacket. A nip in the air felt just right. Lü Yan craned his neck like a duck whose ass got caught in the door. He chuckled out an explanation. "His big ass resembles the rear of a Mercedes Benz. And now he's even got a logo ..."

A few years ago, this city had looked different. Now it was a dreamland of steel and cement, with wider roads and larger gaps between buildings. If you stood on one side of the road to look across at the other side, you'd feel like looking at something as remote as in a dream. It had not been like this a few years before. Back then you could hear the owner of the noodle shop across the street gossiping with others outside his shop. In just a few years' time this city had grown apart from you. I always wondered when that process begun.

Lü Yan was playing The Chicago on the CD player. I rolled the car window down further. The brass instruments sounded tender in the humid air. Peter Cetera sang haltingly, "If you leave me now, you'll take away the biggest part of me. Uh uh uh uh no baby, please don't go."

The car pulled up in front of the building. Sisi wanted some grapes from the store across the street. It was drafty near the building. I stepped inside the lobby to smoke and watch the obsequious old guy at the store showing off one bunch of grapes after another to the man and woman whose arms were wrapped around each other's waists as if they were a legitimate couple. The marker lights on a skyscraper were blinking in the distance. The sky to my right was all lit up by the shopping district below. The sky to my left was dimmer because Fuxing Park was a dark expanse at night.

We had rented this apartment on Yandang Road for RMB 15,000 per month only half a year before. Lobster had paid for the first three months, and I had picked up the tab for the next three. For a while all three of us were hard up. Lobster surrendered the lease he held on a Nissan Cedric, but the money saved was soon down the drain. We went bowling at Hotel Equatorial, where we won a bit more from some Taiwanese. We managed through those weeks somehow. We agreed to leave all cash in an unlocked drawer, but if anyone put aside some for himself, who would tell.

This could happen to anyone. Just look at Lao Cao. In his glorious days he leased an entire office building and then sublet to over a hundred companies, which were created either to cheat or to be cheated. But for about half a year before that, Lao Cao sat idly in our apartment day after day, praying for some break. He would sit in a corner of the room and make phone calls to all sorts of guys. For lunch, he either sat at our table or made do with a cup of instant noodle.

A person must have a dozen grand with him at any time. Others may say a gambler never knows whether he's going to win or lose if the game is still on, but that's not what I mean. We knew most people hanging out with us were not filthily rich, but if they could afford a car and an apartment, a hundred yuan bill to each girl at the night club when the night was over, we'd gladly take them in. We'd eat, drink, and be merry. Occasionally "business" was done, too.

Sisi went into the shower. Lü Yan downed another glass of Chivas Regal. He had had quite a few drinks tonight. He tossed the glass away, his eyes rolled around. He muttered like a bird keen on singing to the morning light but slurred by the worm in its mouth. He busied himself arranging pills on top of the PC. Pills rained down from the bottle. He lined them up by color and then swept them out of sight line by line.

The bottle was empty. He turned the bottle. A little matchstick man on the label was waving his arms to show how healthy he was.

He suddenly turned around. "Have you slept with Xiao Mi?"

I was sitting beside the phone, making random calls to wake happy couples from sleep. His question caught me off guard. I denied automatically. "No."

"Lobster said you did."

It was midnight in a rented living room decorated like a decent office. I fell silent for a few seconds like an idiot. Then I told him, "Come to think of it, yes, once, together with Lobster."

Sisi was done with showering. She stuck her head out for Lü Yan. Lü Yan went into their room. I stripped down in the guest bathroom, took a shower, walked into the bedroom next to theirs, climbed into bed, and turned on the VCR. The woman in the video curled her legs around the man's waist where the camera stared. The concave where the man's spine ended was twisting. Sisi had a body like that woman. I dwelt on the thought for a while before falling asleep. I had pulled back the curtain and left the window open. The air outside was wet. Tires screeched from time to time on the road below. Stray cats whined in the Fuxing Park further away.

II

Halfway through the night, I woke up and poured myself half a glass of water. It was scary to awaken at such a time to find yourself alone. It happened to me frequently. I rolled over my stomach and bang, the cozy slumber was replaced by a chilly room whitewashed in Nippon Paint. Such helplessness.

For a while, I had a woman every night. When there is a woman you might wonder if it would be better to have the bed to yourself, but now you feel hollow because there isn't a warm body beside you. When those women fell asleep after sex, their bodies were warmer than usual, warm and soft, marks left by wrinkled bed linen all over.

On second thought, those women didn't matter. They were just who they were. That Madam from Wuhan International Club would immediately pull on her panties to use the bathroom. I would light a cigarette and watch her move languidly across the room, the slack panty caught in the crease of her fanny.

In the past few years, I had developed the habit of sleeping out. It all started with checking into a hotel every few nights. By and by I got used to the humming of the air conditioner. I slept with the TV on but sound off. The ceiling blinked in sync with the TV screen. My mind was there and not there at the same time.

When I couldn't sleep I had a lot of thoughts and resolutions, but they were all forgotten the next morning. I drank the water in the dark, only to find it was some leftover beer. The water glass glistened on the window sill. The beer was stale. I lit a cigarette, turned on the bedside lamp, groped for a book in the night table drawer.

I always leave books where I can lay my hand on—a good habit from childhood. Or maybe it was a bad one? Money and a book were the only two things I brought to the airport. Airport security guards would usually scrutinize my ID card when they saw there was nothing else on me. That showed reading might not necessarily be a good habit. A sensible man going on a trip would bring a bag with clean underwear in it. He could, of course, also bring a book or a magazine, but it would be kept in the bag, not rolled up carelessly in his hand.

I leaned back against the bedstead, my right hand holding the cigarette and my two left fingers thumbing through the book. The one hundred yuan bill was still there. I like using banknotes as bookmarks. They might come in handy if I couldn't even afford dinner. I moved the banknote to about ten pages behind, determined to turn off the light and go to sleep when I saw it again. On the page that just came into view, the keeper finally came to understand dolphin talk. They started to blabber happily in their own language.

How important language is! We are not seeking happiness; instead we are just seeking some language that enlightens. If a woman makes you happy, it's because the light of language has shot through the ambiguity between you and her. Those women who happen to sleep with us at night are just dolphins with idiosyncratic high frequency languages. They may have smooth beautiful bodies, but they can't make us happy.

The hour hand pointed to one, the minute hand had yet to reach ten. I made an effort to think. It must be a little bit over one o'clock in the early morning. At a night cold and wet like lake water, who would know I was thinking about women while holding a science fiction in my hand? Women are easy to come by if you don't think about them. There was one next door. Sisi would do. Sisi would also warm you up. Why did she call herself

Sisi? Sounds like a gay man. I vaguely remembered a gay guy who later opened a bar. I also remembered him sitting on the toilet to pee like a woman.

Back then—back then my life had probably been more chaotic than it was now. Now was much better. Back then I leafed through magazines on a sofa downstairs while some man and woman were wallowing naked in bed in the attics. I hung out with the gang because I fought with another woman every day. Ironically, the reason why I fought with that woman every day was because I hung out with the gang. I still remembered that woman's name, but I wouldn't mention it now, not even when I was alone at midnight. Mentioning it would cloud my mind wet and sticky.

Now I was clean as a pin. My mind was no longer wet and sticky. I had eventually managed to tidy things up. I had stopped fighting with women. I had stopped remembering. As long as that name didn't come to me, I could relax and even recall some dialogue, some smells. Sometimes when I was more relaxed than usual, I could even recall the sensation from my fingertips.

I sat at the bed, my mouth bitter from drinking. The power indicator flickered in the darkness. My memories rushed back triggered by some tunes and smells. I was a 17-year-old living near an antique market, a market stocked with curiously shaped bottles and jars. I was in a second-floor wing room of a *shikumen*-style house. Sunlight streaked in through the curtain. A tinsmith was hammering on and off in the distance.

It happened out of blue. Women are precocious in this aspect, even before they can be called women. Her hint was beyond me: her face almost calm, her body leaned forward just so.

Then she unbuttoned her jeans, pulled down the zip halfway. She asked, "Do you want to brush against it?" To brush against something is an accident. To touch would be intentional. However, even the former was quite a shock to me. I looked at her dumbfounded. It was hard to tell whether her subsequent smile was tender or sarcastic. She grabbed my finger and jammed it inside her panty.

After a long sigh she whispered into my ear, "Once again?"

This time she left my finger on the edge of her panty. Hesitantly, I retraced the route. There was moist around my finger. I couldn't resist the urge to put it under my nose. It smelled a bit sour. I whispered back, "You're sour down there." She laughed in a weird manner, holding my head to her. Later she told me my remarks made her dizzy.

What did I just say? Language. We are with women in order to seek a language. It has nothing to do with how you construct a sentence. I don't know how to explain. But if you speak the right words and sentences, things straighten out. Nevertheless, if you do speak the right thing at the right moment, you're screwed up.

III

The next morning I went to the atrium of the Hilton, where I sat in a wicker chair by the partition. The tableware caught the sunlight flooding in through the glass roof. There was a pancake on my plate, which I didn't care to eat. Too early for food. I smoked and sipped at the grapefruit juice. A foreign woman sat straight-backed across the partition, smoking and drinking coffee.

I was wearing a thin soft black print cotton shirt under a white bomber jacket. The Clarks shoes from Isetan cost me more than two thousand yuan. My tacky ring with the huge diamond glistened in the sun. I didn't buy it, someone left it with me as collateral against the money he borrowed from me. He also gave me a Rolex. I liked these two items. Wearing them made me feel energetic, an energetic fraud.

My cell phone vibrated in the trouser pocket. It wasn't a Motorola. There was only one Motorola model on sale in the Postal and Telecommunications Offices in Shanghai, the 8500. It was too bulky a brick for me to carry, but ideal as a fight weapon. If some scumbags dared to challenge me, slamming it down on the table in front of them would be as effective as two or three bodyguards. Those kids got their mafia education from gangster movies made in Hong Kong. A bulky phone would win their respect. I thought the model should come with a strap. That way people could wear it around the waist or across the back. I had Lü Yan find me a small Nokia and burn my number into it. It fit my trouser pocket. There were two kinds of frauds:

the classy and the déclassé.

The call was from Xiao Mi. If this woman showed up, Lobster would probably be around. I asked as soon as I picked up, "Is Lobster back?" She said he would arrive in the evening, but she would like to see me at once.

Xiao Mi told me on the phone that Lobster, instead of going back to our apartment on Yandang Road, needed a room in a quiet hotel. I called the receptionist on duty at the Hengshan Hotel, who told me local Shanghai residents were not allowed to take a room. I flirted with her and then pleaded some, saying my pregnant wife could hardly stay at home where people from the housing management office were busy fixing our wind-devastated roof. Amused, she said OK but no next time. I promised to pick up the key at noon.

Lobster must have gotten himself into trouble again. If he couldn't go back to Yandang Road, it meant big trouble. There was no point stressing the word "quiet" to me. I got it! If he couldn't go back to Yandang Road, then neither could he stay at Hotel Equatorial, Hua Ting Hotel or any other new hotel with a straightforward layout. Some hotels might seem quiet, but accommodated interesting clientele, like prostitutes, drug addicts or gamblers. He couldn't use those hotels either. The West Wing of the Jin Jiang Hotel, the two-story building along the Maoming Road, was a better choice. There was no lift or lobby, but easy access through several entrances opening onto the street. Plus, it was an old hotel, where the staff had seen enough to keep cool.

The Hengshan Hotel, known as I.S.S. Picardie Apartments to the old timers, was nice too. The good old Picardie was where paint peeled off, where corridors constituted a labyrinth, and where I had slept with many women. The lifts were located in such a haphazard manner that a newcomer wouldn't find the right lift to reach your room even if he knew your room number. If you took the right lift to the right floor, you would still have to push through a door that led into a hallway and then walk down it to reach your room. People with a secret felt safer here. The maid must call up first before cleaning your room, because she needed you to open the door to the room as well as the door to the hallway from inside. Of course there were additional perks, like a high ceiling, a huge bath, black steel windows with a view of the layered foliage in the Hengshan Park, a glass water flask, woolen slippers, and wall paper with floral patterns.

I took a deep drag on my second cigarette this morning before stubbing it out. White smoke curled up. Xiao Mi materialized behind it. The sun shone on her light brown cheeks, a wisp of white smoke dispersed from her jaw and her ears. I focused on the hollow between her collarbones for about ten seconds, or maybe less—until the smoke was gone. I said, "You're good at tracking people down. I was waiting for you to call me from the entrance."

I told her to help herself to some of the buffet breakfast. When she returned with food, I asked right away, "What had Lobster done this time? Why do I have to run errands for him?"

"I don't know. We were not together."

"Was he in Wuhan?"

"Ask him yourself."

Neither of us spoke in the next few minutes. She buried herself in food and I smoked my third cigarette. I found it hard to strike up a conversation with Xiao Mi when Lobster was not around. When Lobster was around, the two of us could laugh and talk, sometimes we even flirted a bit. I didn't try to put on an act, or, as they phrased it, "to follow the code of conduct." According to the latter, one shouldn't flirt with a friend's girl. It sounds nice, but it is just bullshit.

We used to eat and sleep in the same apartment. We used to share a bathroom. When I woke up during the night, my bare feet often got tangled up in Xiao Mi's dirty underwear as I stumbled through the living room towards our bathroom. But we had always been polite to each other, especially when we were alone.

That summer, we often went to a restaurant on Urumqi Road around eleven or twelve at night. It was around that period of time that having morning tea like the Cantonese was suddenly out among the loafers in the city, whereas midnight snacking caught on. Deep into the night, they would materialize from all corners of the city to gather in a few night snacking places known in the circle. Money was said to flow in freely to owners of such eateries that had karaoke included. Cooked rice soaked in boiled water with pieces of green and some prawns cost you fifty yuan. The restaurant we went to was our favorite. Its owner was a skinny old guy with slender fingers, which wiggled, crossed, and circled in the air as he talked, making us all giddy. If he aimed at convincing you, his fingers would play even more tricks.

The restaurant manager was a girl, though, known as Xiao Mi. She had an extraordinary relationship with the owner. An "extraordinary" relationship is not a "sexual" relationship. I haven't figured out yet whether they slept together. Lobster might not have any idea either.

By "extraordinary", I mean, the owner somehow gave Xiao Mi away as a gift to Lobster, and a valuable gift at that, in return for a favor.

Here is how. Some scoundrels from Yangpu District were so offended by the owner that scores of them would come in at six every night, order just a pot of tea, and sat there until two in the morning. Seeing real patrons scared away and no money come in, the old guy asked around in order to find someone from the neighborhood who got along with the gang from Yangpu. He found Lobster.

So we frequented the old guy's restaurant every day. When business was slack, Lobster would invite Xiao Mi to come over and have a drink. He had agreed to mediate for a fee, but the old guy shortchanged him afterwards. Probably he considered Xiao Mi as part of the payment. Lobster didn't complain. And Xiao Mi became his girl.

Our taxi was stuck on Huaihai Road. According to the driver, it was ten-thirty in the morning, but things would improve in half an hour. I felt restless on the passenger side. It was a narrow street where buses and trolleys rumbled towards us with an apparent intention to kill, and where bicycles needled through the traffic before we were hit head on. I observed that buses were the most ruthless creatures on Shanghai streets, unlike what you found in Beijing. The taxi driver agreed, saying that was because Shanghai bus drivers had their company paying for damages.

To our left was Maison Mode. I spotted Xiao Mi tilting her head to look at the window display in the rearview mirror, so I suggested that we get off, look around inside, and hail another taxi in half an hour's time. Someone jammed the car door the moment we planted our feet on the ground. The world was just like that. People would scramble to fill in where you've just left for too much trouble.

It was a fine day. Maison Mode was a fancy department store. The shop assistants weren't snobbish enough though. They should have cultivated a taste for wealthy clients only and turned a blind eye to gawkers. They shouldn't have addressed each and every visitor with such nice smiles. In a couple of years, they would make some headway.

Xiao Mi couldn't move away from a dress peddled to her by a saleswoman. I reached for the price label, took a look, and told her to try it on. The saleswoman immediately turned the heat on me. Instead of a verbal response I just smiled like a wealthy man without a care in the world. This trick worked. Women felt intimidated in such shops. They found the solid presence of a man with an imperturbable smile very comforting.

Regret hit me with Xiao Mi in the fitting room. Why did I fawn on women like a hotheaded young man? Why did I try to impress on them dependable? But anyway, I would charge it to Lobster later, so who cares.

My cell phone rang. Lü Yan greeted me with curses on the other end. It turned out that some people had stormed into our apartment on Yandang Road, woken him up, and demanded to see Lobster. It took me a while to figure out that he was actually cursing Lobster. I interrupted him, "Who are they?"

"How would I know? Cops. Plainclothes."

"Fuck. Give the phone to their Captain Diao[1]."

Lü Yan roared with laughter. He said Captain Diao couldn't take phone calls because he had been shot on the ass by communist soldiers. I retorted that since Captain Diao rode a bicycle, there was no way for him to get shot on the ass. He said Captain Diao happened to lift his ass from the saddle to fart when the bullet flew in. We ping ponged back and forth. The sales girls who overheard us giggled. They must have seen through me at the same time.

I hung up without promising to return to our apartment. Instead I told Lü Yan to play host to Captain's Diao's men because I was busy. I made several rapid inferences as I put the phone back into my pocket. The situation was not that desperate in our apartment, otherwise those plainclothes police wouldn't have allowed Lü Yan to use the phone, let alone Lü Yan's rowdy language. If they were local police, they would have presented a search warrant, if only to scare targets into submission. If they were civil, they must have come from out of town and had yet to inform their Shanghai colleagues.

Some creditor might have sued Lobster. The police were here to enforce the court order. They would remain polite until they got Lobster tucked away in their van. On second thought, this was interesting. Instead of lying in ambush, the policemen just announced to everybody who they wanted and even allowed phone calls. I decided to pop in.

---

1 Captain Diao is a character in *Shajiabang*, one of the eight model Beijing operas during the Cultural Revolution. He was captain in a Chinese puppet army taking orders from the Japanese during China's War of Resistance against Japanese Aggression (1936–1945). —*Trans.*

IV

Xiao Mi came out of the fitting room like a female secret agent emerging glamorously from a broom closet into the ballroom. I was so carried away that I used my own credit card instead of Lobster's. Remorse seized me as we got into a taxi. I dialed through to Lobster. "Your girl went into an expensive store without any money on her. I paid over three thousand yuan. We'll get it settled tonight."

"Cut it out. Whose girl is she anyway?"

It suddenly occurred to me that I still owed Lobster money back when we played bowling at Hotel Equatorial. The tinge of regret developed into a pang. After pulling up near the Yandang Mansion, I got off the car to check out the surrounding. There was a white Toyota Previa around the corner with a license plate from Jiangxi Province in which someone was lying low. I bared my teeth happily in that direction as a kind reminder: hey comrade, take better cover.

I tried to warn Xiao Mi in the elevator. "Don't tell the cops you're Lobster's girlfriend. Otherwise they may take you away if they can't get hold of him."

"Don't insult the police."

"Well you go ahead and tell them you're Lobster's girlfriend. Let's see how they act."

There were three strangers seated in the living room. The two younger ones both wore Montagut T-shirts, which made them hicks. One even had a gold necklace. The eldest one was talking to Lü Yan. Sisi was leafing through some magazines at Lobster's large desk by the window. All heads turned as we went in.

"Are you Wang Xiaolong's girlfriend?" The oldest cop grinned at Xiao Mi.

Lü Yan chirped up, "She is a girl friend to many people. She's got lots of boyfriends, cops included."

Everybody burst out laughing. Xiao Mi made her way into the bedroom in a few strides without saying a word. From where I sat the view was unblocked. She opened the closet, hung her new dress, and spoke up to the policemen in the living room. "Is he in trouble?"

"Oh yes, big trouble. Wang Xiaolong drew our attention. We don't travel often on business."

I sneered. While Lü Yan handled the "good cop", it was my job to see to the "bad cop". A poker face and indifference were what I needed.

The young man wearing the gold necklace flexed his index finger at me. He pretended to suppress his rage. "You think it's funny?"

I countered by a burst of anger. In a minute I was on my feet and demanding loudly, "Who are you?"

"Police."

"Say whatever you like. Show me your ID."

"Of course we've got IDs. If necessary we can pull out a search warrant or a detention warrant. Do you really want to see them?"

The oldest policeman intervened, "Hey man, stay cool. We're just doing our job. Lobster—is that what you call him? He is in big trouble. You'd better stay out of this. That's the best for you."

The guy wearing the gold necklace pounded the desk on cue as he jumped up. "Don't ask for trouble! I can pull open this drawer and build a case on you if I want to. I'm being nice now. If you don't cooperate, I will bring you in, and in two hours you'll be on your knees begging me to become nice again."

Lü Yan took out a packet of Chunghwa cigarettes from the drawer. Everyone got a cigarette. The oldest police pulled hard at his contentedly and then smiled. "You're having a good time. Such expensive cigarettes."

I lit my State Express 555 and smiled back. "Stop pretending to be an old boar. You police have seen the world. We earned our money the hard way. Look at you. Not everybody can afford to drive a Toyota Previa."

"Cut it out. You call that a hard way to earn money? You're just a bunch of swindlers with a briefcase full of business licenses."

"Sir, you're wrong there. We are not bad guys. We're just businessmen seeking a profit. We often can't even cover our cost."

"Speaking of which, is there a plywood shortage in Shanghai? You've contacts everywhere. Can you help? A relative of mine runs a furniture factory. "

"Easy. Get your money order ready. There is a ship recently arrived from Indonesia. Deliverable in either Shanghai or Guangzhou."

"You are not trying to cheat me out of my money, are you?" He acted like an old rogue, grinning at me and then turning towards the two young men.

Gold Necklace nodded. "For sure. They lie all the time."

Acting as if on self-defense, I craned my neck at Lü Yan. "Lü Yan, show them a copy of that warehouse receipt."

"Hear that. A copy. Heaven knows how many copies of the same warehouse receipt are circulating in the market. I guess there is a pile in each briefcase company in Shanghai."

Lü Yan laughed. "With a deposit I'll show you the warehouse."

"Ha, ha! It's daring of you to cheat the police."

The plywood contract had become a national legend. There was no plywood at all, but millions of RMB changed hands.

Maybe there were some real pieces of plywood, but I had never seen any. The story I heard went like this: someone presented his money order at a warehouse. No sooner had a truck been loaded than the warehouse keeper decided to call it a day. After agreeing to come back the next morning, the buyer was invited to some wining and dining plus karaoke. The next morning, when he woke up, the seller's phone was disconnected, the warehouse refused to deliver, and the money order had been cashed. What happens next differ story from story, but the gist was the same. The buyer would press the seller for delivery for a fortnight or so before it dawns on him that there would be no delivery at all. So he wanted his money back. The seller would agree to a refund, but not immediately. Maybe twenty thousand yuan this month, thirty thousand yuan two months later, and the last payment a few good years later. With other people's money in hand, the so-called seller could make some investment of his own, like a night club or an office complex. If he was agile enough, he could recover the capital plus several times of profits in a couple of years. With several similar tricks he could make a fortune and brag about his legendary first pot of gold.

Lobster was much better at this than I was. You could compare him to an expert poker player who dominated the game, playing his hand precisely and effectively. You might still be in the dark as to why he played that first card when the game was over and he had won all the stakes. According to Lü Yan, Lobster would first decide which card to play the last and then back fold to the first one. As a result his moves were always superior. However, according to Lü Yan, I was good too. I knew all the tricks, but I played to get high, not to get maximum profit. Lü Yan's theory was beyond me.

The nonsensical talk got us on more friendly terms. Xiao Mi made some noise in the bedroom. She had probably dragged a chair to sit in. The oldest policeman leaned towards the bedroom. "I say, young lady. You'd better call Wang Xiaolong right now. Tell him to come forward. It's the best for all of us."

Xiao Mi retorted from inside, "I'm fine now."

"It would be better if you call him. Seriously, don't let him run wild out there. Men should mind the rules when they do business. If they don't, they won't mind breaking a few more rules elsewhere. You do know he has girlfriends in our place, don't you?"

I showed my appreciation for the oldest policeman. "You're good. You know what's on the mind of women. Do you lead the trade union and women's association at your police department?"

He replied cheerfully, "It's true. We checked the hotels he stayed. The rooms were taken under the name of a woman. We're looking for that woman too."

The guy was playing a dirty trick, but I couldn't tell whether it worked on Xiao Mi, at least not at that moment.

V

Around lunch time we parted company with the police. After more than two hours in our apartment, they must have seen what they wanted to see. As we rode the elevator down together, Lü Yan even invited them to lunch, which they declined. After lunch, Lü Yan asked Xiao Mi when we left the restaurant, "Is Lobster in Shanghai or not?" Xiao Mi said no.

Xiao Mi was wearing the dress I paid for, which seemed to draw me closer to her. That, plus all the food and the sun outside, somehow made me feel weird. Come to think of it, Lü Yan cast me a quick glance when Xiao Mi confirmed Lobster was not in Shanghai. Since Xiao Mi stood ahead of me for the taxi, her calves came into view. They were pale in the sun. Her skin was in fact brownish, not fair, but the sun created the illusion. Although I have seen many nude women, only one of them never fades from memory. That was a fair young body with fluff along the calves. Upon closer look there were fine pores on the fair smooth skin.

Thanks to her, I had developed some peculiar taste for women. I had been conditioned to check out women meticulously. I had led a loose life. If you always check out women meticulously, you'll be hard to satisfy, and you'll find the woman with you hardly perfect.

I followed Xiao Mi into the backseat of the taxi. When she got in, I caught a glimpse of a scratch on a raised vein in the hollow of her knee. Distracted, I rolled down the window to smoke.

We sat at the bar on the ground floor of the Hengshan Hotel. We had called Lobster once we got the room key. He said he would arrive at the Shanghai Airport at around five in the afternoon. I decided to kill the three hours or so in between right here. The light was dim, the bar was almost empty.

I sat drinking in a corner. My mind went elsewhere. Xiao Mi was on a bar stool singing into a mike. Her head bobbed, her profile turned towards me. At high pitches her body bent backwards, her neck stretched.

By the time Xiao Mi came toward me smiling and the music went into crescendo, I was a bit giddy after two quick drinks. I clapped my hands haphazardly. Suddenly she sat down and grabbed my left hand to join the clapping. Slow as I was, her hand remained in mine for quite a while.

Despite the drinks my head was clear, very clear. I could come up with a hundred ways to seduce this woman, a hundred quick ways. If you use quick ways, they may work or not work, but they won't get you in trouble, at least not big trouble. Sometimes it's okay to sleep with a friend's girl. If the friend objects afterwards, it was not your fault. Your friend may have many girls. How could you figure out whom you could sleep with and whom you couldn't lay a finger on? The key is to use quick ways, so quick that your friend wouldn't even notice.

However, I sensed this woman was somehow different. She might get me into trouble. Although I had a hundred quick ways, I seemed to be playing a game of deliberation. I was sober, wasn't I? If you seduce a woman in a deliberate way, things might grow complicated.

Xiao Mi was speaking to me. She wanted a cigarette. I fished out two with my lips, one in each corner of my mouth. After lighting up the one in the left corner, I passed it to her. We sat smoking without talking for a while. I grew tense moment by moment, so much so that I could smell it from my shirt collar. I wanted to gather her into my arms and bury her head in my shirt collar for her to smell it too. Yet the alcohol had probably blunted me. I simply reached out a hand to pat her left knee.

The small smooth round kneecap moved slightly under my palm. Xiao Mi had lifted her left leg onto her right before I could retract my hand. As a result, an onlooker, for example the old Taiwanese guy seated at the table in front of us (who wore a sun hat indoors), might assume it was me who grabbed Xiao Mi's knee and crossed her legs.

I couldn't very well retract my hand right then, otherwise I would be rude. My hand had to stay where it was a few seconds longer, and the timing must be perfect. Neither could it make any movement, not the slightest movement. At the same time I must look into her eyes.

Xiao Mi giggled abruptly. She was all smiles. "You look like you're in a movie."

Exactly. I looked like I'm in a movie. Have I mentioned it before? With language that enlightens, the dark hazy terrain which you prepared to grope through is suddenly lit up. All inhibitions vanished. My fingers tightened around her kneecap just once, and then they were withdrawn.

"You look like you're in a movie. Adorable, though. I've never met a man who looks like he's in a movie."

It was three thirty-five. Lobster would exit the airport at around five-twenty. It might take him an hour and a half, even two hours, to make it through the rush hour traffic to the hotel. However, if I took Xiao Mi up to the room right now, we might need an hour, and then at least another hour for the maid to clean up. The idea of timing got me tense again. I needed a trip to the toilet to relieve myself. As I stood up I pecked at Xiao Mi's cheek. She was caught by surprise.

I had an idea on my way out of the toilet, an idea to save myself an hour's time, or less than an hour, because it took about five minutes to get another room at the reception. I hoped there was no guest waiting to be checked in. I also hoped the receptionist who had given me a room before was still on duty. I couldn't afford to leave Xiao Mi at the bar for long.

Despite the drinks I was level-headed. I knew if I went back to the bar after getting another room, the two of us would beat around the bush some more while the clock was ticking. Moreover, I might screw up because of the tension.

I went directly to the new room once the receptionist gave me the key. In the elevator I checked my watch. Less than five minutes had passed. As soon as I opened the door I called Xiao Mi. "I'm in Room 6013." I'd planned it all out. If she made a fuss on the phone, asking affected questions like "why are you there?" or "what do you want me for?", I'd give up today, maybe once for all. For years I'd tried to manage the tension. It made me queasy.

VI

Lü Yan had always said I was a good poker player. The key
to playing a good hand is not to succumb to tension. Men
needed tension from time to time, but too much tension would
ruin the chances. I was way too tense today. Everything had
gone well except for one important thing: I had forgotten to
buy a packet of Durex condoms from the Picardie Shop in the
lobby. I could have bought a regular pack, which made me
unimaginative, or a fruit-flavored pack, which made me a man
of good humor. But I would definitely not buy the so-called
"Pleasuremax"—those ribbed and dotted condoms.

I didn't realize the mishap when Xiao Mi walked in.
The Hengshan Hotel had a policy of not checking in guests
bearing Shanghai ID's, but I had been lucky enough to find a
sympathetic receptionist. Although I was nervous, I had made
all the right moves, and my luck had held. I patted Xiao Mi on
the knee awkwardly. She lifted her leg immediately so that my
hand "stuck" to her knee.

Yet I had forgotten to buy condoms. I took Xiao Mi into
my arms the moment she came inside the room. A pungent
smell of tension rose out of my shirt collar. As I hugged her she
must have taken it in fully. She must have been aroused, because
she gave off a similar smell. There was something else, the smell
of perspiration. Even though I maxed up the air conditioning,
the smell of perspiration was still there. Fresh perspiration. The
moment it came into my nostrils, I pictured in my mind her

moist pores, the thin layer of clear moisture in her armpit and on her abdomen. There should be more perspiration above her ribs where her breasts started to rise.

I didn't think of condoms until I stripped myself bare.

Afterwards we lied wasted in bed sharing a cigarette. A moment before, when Xiao Mi gasped uncontrollably, my right palm closed around her bottom, the fingers stuck uncomfortably into the wound-like slit between her two cheeks. I felt her wriggle in my palm, shifting more and more weight onto it, as if she would like to sit on it. Then came the orgasm.

My fingers hurt. They had been numb when she fetched a towel from the bathroom, wrapped it around my penis, fondled it until it soiled the towel. Now they hurt.

"You aren't as sophisticated as they said you were." Xiao Mi stuck the cigarette into my mouth.

"I'm very sophisticated."

"You're good, but not as sophisticated as they said."

"Why?"

"You forgot the condom. If you have had many women before, as they said you have, you won't forget."

"I have had plenty of women. But I never buy condoms."

I told her the truth, but Xiao Mi wouldn't believe me. I had never bought any condom on my own. I had used many condoms. Every time a woman took out a colorful pack from her purse, I would ask for a look. Sometimes I thought it told a lot about the woman. As a rule they wouldn't buy the ribbed and dotted ones. If they looked forward to sleeping with you, they would buy Durex Extra. On the contrary, if the package read "Featherlite Ultima", they didn't care who they slept with. Only those women with a particular sense of humor would buy fruit flavored condoms. Women into lemon flavor must take a shower immediately afterwards. Women preferring strawberry flavor slept before the shower.

In retrospect it was that woman who had led me astray. My first woman. I was seventeen back then. She was seventeen too, but she knew more. In my eyes she knew everything. We were together for three years. Since year two we made out naked. For two years, we often hid in my rundown apartment on weekends or we would even play truant on weekdays. We stripped ourselves, we made out, but we never had sex. I mean, we would arouse each other with hands or mouth. That was it. As a result I had no idea of condoms when having sex with other women. We had tried many tricks except for the real thing. It was not my fault. I had had no clue. I just followed her instructions. Therefore when I was later with other women, they thought me extraordinary, sophisticated on one hand and naïve on the other.

However, after I learned to use condoms, I no longer felt like performing the things she taught me. I had learned a lot during those two years. As soon as her eyes grew misty, I would hug her tightly and my hands would cover her slit from both the front and the back. I had also learned to seat her on a sofa, bury my head over her lower abdomen, brushing my nose and lips against her hair. At the same time my arms encircled her waist, or a hand simply went under her bottom squeezing her closely. In a short while I would feel her wriggle and her bottom would press my fingers pale. When she stood up, there would be my finger prints. I never did these with any other women, who simply ask me to put on condoms.

If Xiao Mi had taken a pack from her purse, I would have put a condom on and take a shower afterwards. If time allowed, maybe I would have used another one. Things would be much simpler. But now they were not. Now Xiao Mi thought I was good, but not sophisticated. Since she was in no hurry to get up, we kissed from time to time, on the lips, between puffs. When she had the cigarette, I would lower myself to kiss her belly and lay my head on it. She would pass the cigarette to me, and I would blow a white smoke ring around her belly button. Through the white ring I could see a tiny dent which was her belly button. Her belly protruded out a bit around the belly button. I didn't like women with a flat abdomen, because the rib cage would show. A woman on her back with a slightly bulging belly was more comfortable a sight.

Now I was at ease. For a while I had been tense, so tense that I was beside myself. Once at ease, I realized that things wouldn't be as simple as I had thought at first. I had thought this would be a one-off affair, like it was with most other women. However, since there had been no condom, it would be different, or at least there must be second encounter. Of course, a second encounter was possible even if there had been a condom, but that was another story.

VII

The fight to Fuzhou was scheduled to take off at 7:15 p.m. It was now 6:35 p.m. The two of them were easy to spot in the sparsely seated boarding area. I had seen Lobster twice in the past fortnight or so. We hadn't talked much on the night he came back, since everybody was exhausted. A few days later, I went to the Hengshan Hotel to see him. We talked for an entire afternoon, but I left before Xiao Mi returned.

Lobster caught my eyes. He waved while speaking to Xiao Mi with a smile. I smiled back, pointing at the concession stand. Then I went over to buy a packet of State Express 555 cigarettes with some Foreign Exchange Certificates[1]. As I waited for change Lobster went towards the smoking room.

I hesitated before approaching Xiao Mi.

She didn't stir until I stood face to face with her. Then without a word she gestured towards the smoking room.

I said on cue, "Then I'll go for a cigarette too. Can't help it. The rain was too heavy on the way out. All car windows were up. I didn't smoke at all."

There was no need to talk. In the past fortnight we'd seen each other alone a couple of times. We had said enough. Problem was, the thing between us didn't go away. There would be no

---

1   Foreign Exchange Certificate (FEC): a RMB certificate with exchange value rather than a currency, issued between April 1, 1980 and January 1, 1995. Chinese nationals with FEC's to spend were regarded as privileged. —*Trans.*

problem if it just went away. Now I thought it might be a bad idea to accompany Lobster on this trip. If it hadn't happened, or if it had gone away afterwards, I could either go with him or stay at my own will. But now, because of it, I felt obliged to keep Lobster company even though I was ill at ease.

In the smoking room, Lobster was standing near the tarmac peering outside. It was still raining heavily. The rain caught light and the ground glittered. The room was brightly lit except for the strip near windows. On the glass, dark monstrous shadows from outside overlaid with reflections of moving figures inside. Planted on the boundary between light and shadow, we were like dangerous characters in an old black and white movie, two smoking men who knew the worlds of both heroes and villains. Behind them loomed a mysterious woman.

"You didn't tell me she was going with us."

"Does it bother you?"

"No. Just that you might want me to cover you again."

That was the wrong thing to say. It put me on defense. Moreover, the pronoun "she" didn't feel right. It came alive in this smoky glass-walled room, bonding Lobster and me together in a way that had never happened before.

Lobster had used to reveal lots of details when he first carried on with her, like he did with every other new woman. "Fuck, I didn't give until the third go." "I had to enter from behind to get all the way in." He seasoned his casual comments with lewd laughter, as if sex couldn't gratify him unless it was shared. No gentleman would talk like that, although upon hearing it I could well imagine the woman kneeling on the edge of a bed, her face buried in the pillow, her hair all rumpled up, and her ass higher up towards him. By no means a gentlemen, I somehow found such dirty talk brotherly.

The pronoun "she" re-created that sense of lewd brotherly intimacy. It was a tacit provocation, a response to all the sex stories Lobster had shared before.

Only the two of us were left in the smoking room. We

turned to stand against the rail. She was seated on the other end of the boarding area beside two sturdy men from the north. Despite the powerful air conditioning I could feel the warmth of her body, as if we were still tangled nakedly together, belly against belly, my hair down there long and straight, hers all curly.

"I shouldn't have brought her." Lobster waved the cigarette her direction before sticking it back between lips. He spoke as he blew a ring, "Women are troublesome. I heard someone in Fuzhou wanted a word with me."

It took about twenty seconds, ten seconds longer than usual, for his words to actually hit me, because I was preoccupied with going over our itinerary in Fuzhou. Would there be an opening for me, for example, an afternoon when Lobster didn't need company? Suddenly I wanted such an opening badly, especially in Fuzhou, right under Lobster's nose. The idea excited me so much that the muscle on my abdomen contracted in spite of myself.

My fantasy ran wild as I kept my apparent cool. The idea of slipping my hand under her blouse when Lobster was talking to someone in the room next door aroused me. Lobster turned to give me a look before continuing his talk. Now I was all ears. He said, "With you I'm more at ease. If case something happens, the two of you can get out together."

"What could happen over there?"

"I'm not sure about Lao Chen. Do you remember the gang from Fuzhou last year? The guy we kicked out of the South Huating Guesthouse? I heard they were on good terms with Lao Chen."

"You mean Lao Chen set up a trap in Fuzhou for us?"

"I'm not sure yet, but I must keep an eye on him. Don't worry. He won't harm me in Fuzhou. You just take care of her."

In our circle you should never trust a person one hundred percent; neither should you expect others to always keep their promises. The funny thing was you still made agreements with them. Even if you suspected that Lao Chen lured you to Fuzhou on purpose, you had to go there. Because you never knew. He might plan to harm you, but what next? Would he cooperate with you next? Of course, I was referring to the bigger circle. Within the bigger circle you should maintain an inner ring of trustworthy friends, like the one formed by Lobster, Lü Yan, and me.

Lobster suddenly laughed out loud. "Who knows? You should probably bring a woman to Fuzhou too. We take two rooms anyway."

"Why bother? Women are the same everywhere."

"No they're not." Lobster waved again in her direction. "Women like that aren't there for you to pick."

I wondered whether to follow up on this comment or not, but before I made up my mind Lobster spoke again, "Lü Yan told me that you're interested in Xiao Mi. Is that so?"

Was there a glint in his eyes or was it the reflection of a course light? It was hard to tell. I grew uneasy in the dark corner of a well-lit hall. Didn't we always share women? Think fast, I told myself, think fast how you had responded to such questions before. Once, on a rainy night like this, in a car driven by Lü Yan, you sat in the back seat and Lobster was on the passenger side talking about a woman he had recently hooked up with. Most probably it was not Xiao Mi, but some other woman. My memory failed there. We were all drunk. Lobster said her pussy was the prettiest he had ever seen. He rolled down the car window, laughing like crazy, bawling and shouting all kinds of adjectives. What did I say then? I said seeing was believing. How did Lobster answer me? He said brothers came first, and all of us would have a look eventually.

It was time to board before I came up with a response.

VIII

I sat idly at the lobby bar of the Overseas Chinese hotel. I had been idle in Shanghai too. That was why I had immediately agreed to accompany Lobster to Fuzhou. It had happened many times before. Because I was idle, I took others' suggestions gladly despite the uncertainties. Instead of going all out to get myself busy, I followed unknown paths.

That night, I was shocked, upon arriving at the airport, at the sight of Xiao Mi. When Lobster and I spent an entire afternoon together at the Hengshan Hotel, he didn't mention Fuzhou at all. Two days later, he called. I agreed readily. However, he made no reference to Xiao Mi.

I had brought a thick novel with me to the airport in anticipation of sitting around all day at some Fuzhou hotel. I thought I might finish the novel because my only role was to contribute some idea that others would most probably ignore. I had been relaxed, thinking this was just like moving from one hotel to another for a change, until my eyes fell on Xiao Mi at the airport. Xiao Mi was the uncertainty. My feelings were mixed. I was agitated.

Indeed, things span out of control as soon as we reached Fuzhou. For a starter, we were held up at the Fuzhou Airport for over one hour. Rainstorm in Xiamen had disrupted the entire flight schedule. In fact, the streak of misfortune had kicked in when we were still in the air. The turbulence was so vehement that flight attendants made repeated requests that everyone buckle up. Passengers piling out of delayed planes created more congestion on the ground. Bunches of them crowded around taxis arguing who had priority. It took our taxi another one hour and a half to reach the Overseas Chinese Hotel downtown, because all vehicles tried to cut in front of all other vehicles and consequently four-lane traffic became eight. It was almost eleven at night when we arrived.

It was my job to check in and Lobster's to make a round of phone calls. Thanks to the unexpected delays, all appointments fell through. Lao Chen claimed on the phone that he had been waiting at the hotel lobby between nine-thiry and ten-thirty. The Taiwanese guy we were supposed to meet had to drive overnight to Fuqing. We had to wait for him to come back.

The next two days came to a complete standstill. We attended numerous meals and Lobster made phone calls non-stop. When there was free time I slept in my room. Lao Chen would show up at night fall with a bunch of guys who looked different but behaved similarly. After two days I felt I had met half of all hustlers in Fuzhou. We went to all kinds of night clubs to drink, throw dices and do finger-guessing games. I won repeatedly in a finger-guessing game in which you used different finger combinations to form numbers ten, fifteen, and twenty. Xiao Mi was my only match. The two of us ended up playing against each other, for which I almost got us both drunk. Lobster even made a hue and cry for us to change the stakes from money to stripping. He said after each round, the loser should remove one piece of clothing until there was none. However, a debate arose as to whether we could keep our underwear. In the end we didn't revert to new rules of game.

We were carried away with all the merry-making. On several occasions, I stole kisses from her when Lobster left the hotel room for a few minutes. Once, the three of us returned to the hotel together. Lobster wanted to use the business center to send some faxes. The two of us went up to the room without him. As soon as I latched up I pressed her against the back of the door with my knees and my lower front. She was almost lifted off her feet. Her response was lukewarm, but I was all fired up.

Before bedtime last night, Lobster called me. I could overhear the two of them flirt with each other, so I cursed and hung up. I read some more of the novel. Lobster called again when I was ready to turn in. I checked the time. About an hour had elapsed. I spoke to him, "Are you done? Get some sleep." Lobster chuckled on the other end. "Xiao Mi has something to show you."

Xiao Mi was knocking at the door before I hung up. I let her in. She wore slippers barefoot. There was an illustrated magazine in her hand. I turned round to lie in bed. In an instant I had realized that was a porn magazine from Hong Kong. Between the door and the bed, all kinds of thoughts flashed across my mind, some of which were instantaneously dismissed as delusion— Lobster wouldn't mean it even if he really appreciated a friend. I decided he just wanted to take advantage of my sleepiness to play a prank. I leaned back against the pillows and half hid in the shadow cast by the night lamp. I looked at her with what I assumed to be a sad smile.

Abruptly she jumped into the bed. Hands against the wall, she towered over me. She wanted to straddle me but her knee length blue and white checkered nightgown tripped her. I reached out to support her. Her free hands immediately lifted the nightgown up to her neck. With her knees free, she knelt with a thump on the pillows. My head was between her thighs, my ears squeezed. A tuft of curly hair brushed against my jaw. My eyes were so close to her lower abdomen that I could see blue veins underneath her skin and a light brown mole growing out of the hair roots.

A warm acid smell permeated my nose. I was dizzy. All I was conscious of was her suppressed raving. "But I wanted to be with you ... But I wanted to be with you ..."

Afterwards, I had difficulty falling asleep. By three in the morning, the sky turned into an inexplicable deep blue. A door seemed to close down the corridor. Cars honked in the street. Bicycle bells rang. Doubt crept into my mind.

Suddenly I was wide awake. Maybe the reason why she had complied with Lobster's proposal and delivered the magazine with strangely posed Southeast Asian women to my room was to tell me that nothing had happened between Lobster and her in that hour. Indeed, nothing had happened. There was still a trace of that fresh warm smell in my nose.

The magazine was lying open on the floor. I could see a color photo of a woman's private parts taken from top down. Last night, around three in the morning, when I could hardly sleep, I flipped to lie on my belly near the edge of the bed, gathered the sheets between knees, reached out my left hand to browse through it. Faint blue light shone through the window. My hand stopped on this page. My mind was in a whirl.

It was now two o'clock in the afternoon. I sat in the hotel lobby having no idea how to kill the time. After lunch I had strolled around Fuzhou on my own. I went into the Friendship Store known for fleecing tourists to pore over the surface of a pair of lacquer vases looking for air bubbles. A shop assistant came over to peddle them in a tone as if she were chanting ancient Chinese poems. Fascinated by her tone of voice, I bought a pile of fruit bowls and smoking sets as well as the vases. I had her wrap them up and stuff newspapers into the hollows. Not knowing what to do with all these boxes, I went into a post office, filled in many forms, and sent them away to some addresses on top of my mind. I wonder whether any air bubble on the lacquer ware would burst thanks to rough handling on the way to their destination.

It was hot and humid in Fuzhou although it was already October. Having nothing to do and nowhere to go, I sat in the hotel bar drinking a glass of gin tonic, in which the bar tender had added an extra finger of gin. Lü Yan called from Shanghai. He blabbed about for some minutes before making a suggestion, "If have nothing to do down there, buy yourself a ticket and come back to Shanghai."

"There is nothing to do in Shanghai either."

"Lobster told me you are intimate with his girl."

"With whom?"

"Fuck. Are you playing dumb with me? It is true then."

This phone call gave me a vague sense that something was going on behind my back. Someone was talking behind my back. I thought about it for a while. Since it was about a woman, I could very well enjoy myself.

IX

L obster told a story as we rode in a taxi. The driver was
so enthralled that he almost forgot to make a turn at an
intersection until the last minute. He swerved the car violently
as if we were in a car chase in a gangster movie. Suddenly we
found ourselves in a dimly lit side road.

I didn't usually buy this kind of stories. You couldn't pull
out a gun in broad daylight in Taiwan, not in the evening either.
If you shot at the tire of a car just because it had bruised your
car while parking, that was even harder to believe. Such story
line didn't even work for a gangster movie. It might work for a
Kung Fu movie. The story about the prisoner who had jumped
from a ship into the sea was a load of baloney. It was reasonable
for the authorities to put a person away in a remote island prison
for beating people up. It was also reasonable for the prisoner
to grow scared on the way to the island. Any normal person
would be scared by the prospect of digging trenches in rocky
soil with crude tools on a desolate island in the South China
Sea. Everything so far was reasonable, but what came next
was somehow incredible. A prisoner, however scared he was,
couldn't just jump from a ship into the sea. Even if he did, he
could hardly swim all the way back to the mainland. If he did,
that would be a miracle. Moreover, how about the heavily armed
soldiers escorting the prisoners?

Nevertheless, who cares? It was just a story. Didn't people
make a name for themselves by appearing in such stories? They

resorted to violence and intrigue in order to create some stories. Once stories were created, they could live by telling them.

However, according to Lobster, the story was true. We were going to meet the hero tonight at his birthday party. Guests included his friends, underlings and business partners. For the time being he was doing business on mainland China. That was to say, he was living on stories now. People attending the party believed the story and were awed by it. They must believe it or at least pretend to believe it, because in that circle, the nonbeliever invited trouble from the swarm of believers. Once you became a believer you were obliged to teach nonbelievers a lesson. It had been like this throughout the ages. When stories accumulated, they became legends, or sometimes, history.

Half an hour later I saw this legendary figure on the third floor banquet hall of a hotel. The hotel was such an obscure presence on an unlit street that our driver made quite a few turns before locating it. We waited outside the glass door of the hotel for a couple of minutes. It was all dark inside. A chain with a padlock sealed the door from inside. Then a guy appeared. He turned on a light and came over to unlock the door. Lobster exchanged a few words with him. The guy went in. When he came back he showed us in. In the elevator Lobster told me, "This is a hotel. There are rooms on three floors. You can stay overnight if you are drunk."

The banquet hall was right across from the elevator. Several young men stood at the entrance. Inside the hall there were many more people, some of whom Lobster knew. I knew none. The hero in Lobster's story was surrounded by guests in the nave of the hall where sofas were arranged. Lobster brought Xiao Mi and me over. The guy was plainly dressed and soft spoken except for the occasional unbridled laughter.

After that I drank. All liquor was poured into a huge glass tank on a table in the middle of the hall. Lobster had brought two bottles of Royal Salute in a paper bag. As he poured the whisky into the tank he told me, "Each man brings a bottle of liquor. The party won't be over until the tank is dry." In the tank there was a stainless ladle. Tumblers of various sizes scattered around the tank. There was also some food on the tables nearby.

Lobster was pulled aside by someone. Xiao Mi sat among the women. I took a seat alone in a corner by the window nurturing a large tumbler. The liquor in the tank went down by about a third when I finished half of mine. My hearing seemed to sharpen, or maybe the others became louder, but anyway the clamor was raised.

A guy at the next table was telling a story. His voice reached my ears intermittently, "They cornered him on a balcony in Dongguan. He was offered two choices: one was a brick …"

Someone interrupted, "Fuck, what for? To ask him how heavy the brick was?"

"He had two choices: one was to jump off the balcony, the other was to smash his front teeth with the brick. Two front teeth at least. The room was on the sixth floor. He took the brick. At one smash two front teeth fell …"

What happened afterwards? I took a huge gulp. My teeth tingled as the liquor went down. Those stories were all similar. I could predict the ending. What was the ending like? Usually the guy would lie low for a few months. But he was a tough guy. Remember? He smashed his own front teeth. He would lie low until people forgot about him. And then he would stab a knife into the belly of the guy who had passed him the brick.

I wanted to open a window, but I didn't feel like moving. I needed some fresh air. I was dizzy. Someone shook a dice cup before slamming it down on a table.

"Do you know what happened later?"

Go ahead and tell, you fool! I took another gulp.

"Everybody was impressed. Everybody. Who would hurt himself like that? Such resolution. Not the slightest hesitation. Bang! Two teeth fell."

Yes, yes, bang, just like the sound of two dices falling out of the dice cup. I wanted another gulp.

"Everybody was impressed, including the gang boss. The boss praised him. Then he was invited to a banquet. At the banquet the boss gave away his woman to him. The boss said a man like that deserved his girl. He even gave the woman a big chunk of money."

That was another version of the story. Happy ending, no vengeance. Appearances were kept.

"It's not over yet. About a year later, the gang boss was put into jail. What bad luck! His girl ran away with another man, and he himself got imprisoned. Guess what? He heard from an inmate that the two smashed front teeth were false!"

That was a good twist of a story. I lit a cigarette. It turned out that someone in the know had tipped off the guy on the phone.

"He's got his man in the gang. He already knew the boss wanted his two front teeth. He had a fucking dentist replace the two good teeth with false ones. Shit, the dentist was good. Nobody could tell. Anyway, he had help. Plus, nobody could actually see on the balcony at night. His face was a wreck, but who could tell? "

What happened to the two good teeth? Someone asked. What did they go? I drank up and helped myself to another ladle from the tank? I glanced at Xiao Mi. She sat all among other women in the dress I paid for with my Great Wall Card. On my way back to my seat I thought, the guy had better mount the two teeth on a pair of earrings for that woman. In that way he could see them dangling from that woman's earlobe every day. Whenever they dangled his teeth root would hurt. That's the best. He would always appreciate that woman. Every time he fucked her it would hurt. Then he would focus on revenge.

When we left the party that night, Lobster told me the deal was done. Goods would be shipped once the deposit was made. Accounts would be settled every three months. I slumped on the front seat, too drunk to talk. After a while Lobster said, "I'll go to Fuqing with the Taiwanese tomorrow. You two stay here."

The night was tender. Nobody stirred in the car. Xiao Mi made a swallowing sound.

X

The morning streaked through the curtain into the room. I leapt out of bed. My feet landed on some fabric. Looking down, I found myself naked and aroused. My shorts stuck to the ankles. I had a vague memory of how they were peeled down to the knees and then to the ankles last night. But I hesitated a lot before each move, like a woman. Eventually I did nothing to myself.

I didn't sleep well. I felt foggy on my way down to breakfast with Lobster. I should have said no to him on the phone. I didn't need all those cereal, juice, bread, and sausages. What I needed was a good sleep until lunch. My mind would clear up by then, clear enough to think. However, since I had tossed and turned in bed the entire night thinking about his girl, I felt obliged to breakfast with him. Moreover, it would be fun thinking about his girl while discussing serious business matters like deliveries, logistics, and funding.

A half-hearted person like me was seldom high. But once high, my mind worked at high speed despite the lack of sleep. While Lobster was waiting for his omelet I told Xiao Mi, "I missed you all night last night."

"What if he comes back?"

"I'll call him. I'll call him one hour after his car leaves. I'll tell him we are reading a magazine together."

She chuckled. There was some toast crumbs on her lips. She was charming.

"You dirty old man. I've never seen a dirtier man. Can we wait until after lunch? I'll feel better."

"But I miss you. I missed you all night. My body was a letter Y all night."

She wrinkled her eyes and nose laughing. More toast crumbs descended on her lips. She put down her knife and fork to swag her left index finger at me. Before she could make an "O" with her right thumb and index finger, she bent over the table with laughter.

You were just horny. She was just another woman. You asked for all the trouble. I sat staring at the telephone on the night table muttering to myself. She had gone upstairs right after breakfast claiming she needed more sleep. I saw Lobster off at the hotel entrance, sent a fax at the business center, and did some shopping at the hotel shop. Everything was ready, but she wanted to wait until noon. After all those gestures she made me wait.

I was consumed with both anxiety and thrill. I decided to get some sleep. Before that I needed to soak my penis first in hot water and then in cold water. That way I could fall asleep.

No sooner had I stood in the shower than someone knocked at the door. It must be her. A hotel maid would press the doorbell, but Xiao Mi wouldn't. The bell was too formal for an affair.

About ten minutes later, order was temporarily restored to a world that had been upside down in the past three hours.

High as I was, I had made many stupid mistakes. Even so, the world was finally at peace. First, in my frantic rush to tear down her panty, I kicked her toes by mistake and tears welled up in her eyes. Then, I threw myself on top of her. Instead of kissing her my head collided with her nose. On the eleventh hour I remembered the Okamoto condoms. But when I tore the pack open I found they were fake and the wrong size. I put one on anyway. I couldn't wait. Our bodies intertwined like two springs. They wound up tighter and tighter until they snapped.

The condom had slipped inside her. It took me a minute to fish it out. She skipped around the bed like a cartoon chick in a rhythmic gymnastics performance. Then she busied herself in the bathroom for a long time. However, when she came out, she said it might not matter, because she wasn't ovulating.

I was so exhausted that I fell asleep for about half an hour. Before I opened my eyes she was alerted (it was probably because of her hand on my leg).

"You're a fool."

I hummed.

"You are a dirty fool, but I like you."

I responded by another hum. Without opening my eyes I moved her hand slightly away.

"But I still don't know if you have a big heart or not."

I removed her hand from me, flipped over to lie on my belly beside her. My right arm went under her left armpit to caress the little concavity on the back of her neck. My right leg curled up between her legs. I was attached to her like an octopus or a naked rock climber. Someone looking down from the ceiling must find me funny. A patch on my right leg became wet and itchy.

"My heart is big enough," I told her. "I missed you so much last night even though I knew you were with him."

"How did you miss me?"

"I told you. My body was a letter Y all night. I almost used my hand. "

She kissed me once. "What an old hand. Is this how you use your hand—"

She formed an "O" with her left thumb and index finger.

"No. That is how you strangle a person." I grabbed her hand, smoothed out the rest of her fingers, and then folded them loosely into a fist.

"So it is. What an old hand."

She grabbed my hand and repeated my gestures. She said, "Your hand is much bigger than mine. I like it. It's big and capable. Show me how you do it."

"Piss off."

She giggled. I felt too cozy to talk. She went quiet for a while before asking, "Have women ever lied to you?"

"What? Why?"

"I want to know if you're smart enough, if your heart is big enough. So tell me, have women ever lied to you?"

You lied to Lobster last night. You lie to me now. You lied to me last night to make me lie to Lobster today. Men lie occasionally whereas women tell the truth occasionally. In other words, men lie only when lies are necessary whereas women tell the truth only when truth is necessary. Men with a plan would lie. Women with a plan don't tell lies. If a man lies to you, he wants something from you. If a woman lies to you, she wants to give you something. She tosses out some bait thinking she is going to lie to you, but in fact she just wants to toss the bait out. Therefore, a man who lies is dreadful while a woman is dreadful only when she doesn't lie. I have to say, only a big-hearted man like me can sort this out.

But I didn't feel like talking. I just wanted to kiss her and turn my right leg rhythmically.

XI

At noon Xiao Mi insisted on having lunch. I didn't want to waste time. I lingered in bed. My hand reached out to pull down the panty she had just put on from her back. Then I bit her ass. Screaming, she bounced off like a rabbit and almost tripped herself.

We spent an hour in the restaurant, where we even called Lobster. He sounded as excited as he had struck gold. He also said it took less than half a day in a boat to reach Taiwan. If he went there for a few days, could we take care of ourselves? I promised him that we would take good care of each other.

I had to say, I was not as upbeat as Lobster was about the deal this time. The crux of the matter was the one million yuan deposit. Once it was made they would deliver. Accounts would be settled three months later. In other words, if you made the one million yuan deposit, you could take as many deliveries as possible in the next three months. If everything went well, in three months you wouldn't worry about the deposit any more. Your profit would be several times the deposit as long as you could sell two or three shipments in these three months. The resell price was at least double the purchasing cost. That would be windfall profits indeed.

The problem was you had to pay the first one million yuan. There was no shortcut here. If you tried to play tricks despite all the stories you had heard, I had to say you were out of your mind. In other words, your head was a blocked toilet. I wouldn't be surprised if someone cracked your head open with a gun. I would even expect shit splashing out.

For money matters you needed help from Lao Cao. If you were an old friend with collateral, he could help you deceive others "with money from tomorrow", just as promised by a Bank of China advertisement. Of course, afterwards you had to pay him interest. The interest wasn't that high considering the risk. If you borrowed money from him to buy a diamond ring for your girl or to refurbish your apartment, then the rate would be too high. Mind you, Lao Cao refused to finance anything illegal. He had his own set of criteria. You must ensure that, as the conventional clause in contracts went, "all documents are in proper order." That was about it, but it was hard to explain to people not in the know.

Suppose Lao Cao gave secret credit ratings to us, mine would be higher than Lobster's, because I had helped him once or twice when he was down and out, although this wouldn't be significant enough to impair his judgment. However, once a story about you floated, you'd better play by it, right? You ended up playing by the story. In a story about Lao Cao and me, he had to stay loyal to friends who were loyal to him.

I was only too glad to let Lao Cao earn a reputation for being true to friends. It didn't hurt me. But I knew in actual truth the main reason why Lao Cao had been accommodating so far was because, unknown to others, he was helping manage some of my money. Although we were friends, we followed business protocol. What was more; my money was dwarfed by all the other money entrusted to him by those wealthy Zhejiang businessmen. I held no stake in his company. He just arranged discrete loans and paid me regular interests. Lao Cao pinched pennies. I trusted him. You had to make investments through different channels. That was called risk diversification.

I didn't tell Lobster I couldn't help. Neither did I indicate I could. One should always leave decisions to the last minute. That way you have the final say, and others would pave the way for you.

It was like watching things spinning in a centrifugal machine. By and by the unwanted parts would be separated. That was where I was superior to Lobster. That was not something you could learn by hanging out with hustlers. You should read books and use your brain. Lobster was indeed a better poker player than I was, but he hadn't necessarily mastered the art of poker playing. Every player held some trump card. You shouldn't hold onto yours till the end of the game (they should serve a purpose instead), neither should you play offhand. You should time it well and play out your trump card at the stalemate, and then you guide the game to whatever end you desire.

Although Xiao Mi slept with me, her heart was with Lobster. I had no idea what happened between them, but she was increasingly unreasonable. I told her to finish her food sooner, yet she seemed to savor every bite. I tried to flirt with her, praising her good features. She turned a deaf ear. When I flirted some more, she glared at me, as if the novelty had worn off.

To be frank, although I had a crush on her, I hadn't come so far as to decide to confront Lobster. Like always, I preferred to leave the decision to the last minute.

However, the one million yuan was a matter of principle. I would discuss the feasibility of a loan with Lao Cao businessman to businessman, but I would never make him pay for my affair. Therefore, even if Xiao Mi cared about this deal more than ever because of Lobster, I must keep my head. I could tell she wanted me to make some concession to Lobster. Probably she felt guilty. I didn't. A year before I was sleeping with a nurse. When Lobster saw her at one of our dinners, he told me, "Shit, your big ass girlfriend is hot. I want to fuck her." I gave him a smile. Whatever, just don't make me a pimp. Later he fucked her for sure. He even called to break the news. I just laughed it off.

As we went up she insisted on using their room.

"Lobster might call me."

"He will also call me."

"You needn't stay in your room. He can reach your cell phone. I must stay in the room."

He could also reach your cell phone. But I didn't feel like refuting her. There was an entire afternoon of sex ahead of us, why bother? Yet this made me feel guilty somehow. Sleeping in his bed sounded worse than sleeping with his girl.

When Xiao Mi inserted the key my hand went to her crotch. Two men emerged from the other end of the corridor, one thin, the other fat. It was too dim to tell whether they were snickering or their faces were born askew. They reminded me first of Laurel and Hardy, then two columnists who often appeared on TV. The fat guy carried a roll of newspaper, and the thin guy kept his right hand under his shirt. I whispered to Xiao Mi, "Trouble is coming."

In an instant they were in front of us. The fat guy leapt at me. I crashed into the room bringing Xiao Mi with me.

XII

The thin guy showed his right hand. He was carrying a knife. Stars were dancing before my eyes and my ears rang from the collision with the door frame. This was like flash cuts in movies. Once I recovered a bit, I moved muscles on my face. Good, my mouth was not agape like an idiotic moviegoer's. Then I sized up the knife. It was a stainless knife about thirty centimeters in length and four centimeters in width with a black wooden handle. It resembled a watermelon knife you could buy at a grocery store, but the thick back indicated otherwise.

The fat guy drew the curtain before ripping his newspaper open. There was a sword in a sheath engraved with some indistinguishable pattern, like those swords in souvenir shops. I couldn't help laughing although it was not the best time.

My grin froze as concussion befell me. There was a loud noise and my earflap burned. My eyes had captured images like a high-speed camera. They were now replaying the fat guy's moves in my mind's eye. I saw him raise the sword in slow motion and then hit my shoulder without unsheathing it. On its way down the sword grazed my ear.

I also had a glimpse of a look of pity on Xiao Mi's face. She uttered a short cry.

I felt myself a complete idiot. I should have been more alert. I shouldn't have thought of Laurel and Hardy upon seeing two guys in a deserted corridor, one with a roll of newspaper and another with a hand hidden beneath clothes. Neither should I have laughed at seeing the sword. I had been way too slow. It was ridiculous to attack people with such a sword though. Even the fat guy agreed, because he withdrew the sword halfway from the sheath. There were grooves along the double-edged sword.

For a split second I thought Lobster had sent them, because after all I had slept with his girl. But I dismissed it immediately. The two guys went on to demand the whereabouts of Lobster. They didn't target me then. After the question they fell silent, as if waiting for someone else or further instructions. Anyway, they behaved as if they had been following a checklist before discovering a blank page with no more instructions. Since it was beyond them to take initiatives, they had to wait.

Tension eased off in the room. They were smoking. I wanted to smoke too, but my left ear burned so much that I gave up. The TV was turned on. It was Star TV news. Some guy drew out a gun from his trench coat to shoot at the White House. The fat guy was impressed.

Their question came back to me. They asked, "Where is Lobster?"

So, they had known I was not Lobster, but apparently they knew who Xiao Mi was. It was reckless of them to have forced Xiao Mi and me into the room. They should have kept stalking. Apparently the mastermind behind this was not a master at all. I considered the two clowns in disdain.

A dozen minutes later, more people came in. The leader looked serious with a Motorola high frequency walkie talkie. I looked at them with new eyes. It was more comforting to deal with professionals. From then on, everybody knew what he was supposed to do and did it systematically. Someone frisked us. He took my wallet and cell phone. We were taken downstairs. Elevators were guarded. Two men escorted Xiao Mi and me. All others fanned out. They walked with an air of self-assurance. The lobby was nearly empty at this hour in the afternoon. Receptionists looked at us curiously. I guessed they were thinking of police making arrests.

I couldn't afford to make any rash move. They had weapons. Those weapons might look ridiculous, but they could kill. I had heard stories. The moral of them were all the same: do as you are told. Several bellboys stood at the hotel entrance. They didn't approach us to make the routine enquiry as to whether we needed a taxi. Taking in their facial expressions I tried to imagine how they would react if I shouted "kidnap". Most probably they would immediately make way for the gang.

Two cars pulled over. We were shoved into the first one, a limo that was a Cadillac or a Chrysler. I hadn't enough time to check before they forced me into the back seat. The two rows of seats were arranged face to face. Xiao Mi and I were seated in the middle with a man on either side. Once in the car they pulled the curtains close and bared their weapons. The leader sat beside the driver. There was a glass partition between Xiao Mi's seat and the driver's. The leader was talking to the driver, but I couldn't hear clearly.

Despite the air conditioning it grew stuff very quickly, for there were far too many passengers. I grew drowsy and less nervous.

The driver slammed the brakes. Jolted, I opened my eyes as if I had slept for ages. Xiao Mi's eyes met mine. All kinds of feelings welled up in my heart. Neither the fat guy nor the thin guy was in sight. They were probably in the other car. Without them Xiao Mi and I would be lying in the hotel bed with the thermostat tuned down. I would pull back the curtain to let the afternoon sun shine on her honey-colored body. The air conditioner would blow out cool dry air constantly and suck away our perspiration. This was not the way it should be at all. Sweat of panic oozed from our skin and stuck to our armpits and crotches. Despite the turbid air mixed with odors from hostile males, I could still smell her perspiration.

I should have had a stronger sense of guilt. I should have insisted on not going to Lobster's room. How could I have looked forward to sleeping with another man's girl in his own bed! In that case the thin guy might not have approached, and the fat guy might not have reached us before Xiao Mi opened the door. We might have entered the room and shut them out. We might be in bed now. My head would be buried on her honey-colored belly, and I would be drinking in the smell of her perspiration.

Surrounded by poker faced men carrying lethal weapons, I suddenly realized my vulnerability. At the same time, I yearned for her body. Her panic nonchalance filled me with a tenderness I had never experienced before.

The car stopped abruptly. The leader got off. A few minutes later, the door on my side was open. Someone outside the car said, "Stay where you are."

The door was slammed close.

A stir went over the crowd inside. We all stretched and changed our posture. I moved my right leg. It was limp and numb.

After a long while the car started again. At a gas station I was taken to the restroom. We went back to the car before Xiao Mi did. We were once again on the road. There was no more stop until it was all dark.

XIII

We were led into a stone house. Its front gate consisted of a row of wooden panels. The far right panel had been removed. All was quiet under the starry sky. The wind was going strong. Since such standalone houses in the countryside usually faced south, I surmised that the wind came from the southeast. The wooden door panels and windows creaked in the wind. I was taken into a room to the left. Before I went in I saw them take Xiao Mi up a wide wooden staircase that faced the front gate. A funny looking ancient bamboo four-poster bed stood in my room. The bamboo strips were already discolored with age. On the other side of bed, a big square table was placed against the wall. Between the table and the bed squatted a chamber pot. The wooden window in the south wall was creaking in the wind, too.

I sat at the table. My guard was kind enough to leave me a packet of cigarette, the exact packet taken from me previously. He sat at the door to talk to his friends outside without forgetting to check on me from time to time. Later, they ate and drank in the living room. A plate of baby squids and an assortment of shellfish were brought to me together with a can of beer.

Doors and windows went on clanging in the strong wind. I slept off and on. Someone, probably the guards, stayed up, because I heard occasional clicks of lighters. They were exceptionally audible in the spacious stone house. Xiao Mi must be sleeping in the room above mine, because by supper time I knew there was no other woman in the house. At midnight I heard someone walk about on the wooden floor above me and then there came the sound of urine into a chamber pot. I could picture her sitting on the chamber pot with eyes half closed and her panty pulled down to the knees. When I urinated into the chamber pot it didn't sound like a trickle.

The next morning I was taken out of the room. When we passed through the living room I found all door panels had been removed and piled against the outer wall. Outside the door was a fenced-in bare courtyard. In the yard there was a tilled patch. Some peanuts showed in the soil. I saw the fat guy and thin guy again. The thin guy was sitting in a bamboo recliner in the sun with closed eyes. The fat guy was looking at me beside the peanut patch. Sunshine cast onto the granite floor of the living room. This was a solid house. Everything except for the wooden doors, windows, beams, and staircases were made of granite.

I was shown into the kitchen to the right of the living room. It was huge. There were two doors and rows of wooden windows in three walls. All windows were thrown open. Outside the east windows were a slope overgrown with green and brown grass. The kitchen range was placed near the north windows. In the middle of the kitchen, stones were laid on top of each other to support a long plank. The leader from yesterday was sitting on a stool near it drinking tea.

There was a kettle on the stove. After water boiled he arranged four small teacups in a tea tray, changed the tea leaves in the teapot before adding boiling water. The first pot of tea was poured over the small teacups to warm them up. The second pot was for us to drink. Aroma rose in the kitchen. He pushed a teacup my way. "Fresh tea picked this fall."

I drank the tea. I smoked. Over the second cup he handed me my phone. He wanted me to call Lobster. When Lobster picked up, I passed the phone back to him.

I knew all the details of the episode they discussed on the phone. In fact it was me who sold the goods seized by Lobster at that parking lot on Caobao Road. Lobster had followed all protocols. If others violated the protocols, of course he could return like for like. Some people might say Lobster had trapped them by playing dumb. If that was the case, they deserved it.

In our circle, protocols sometimes overrode ownership. If the rightful owner of goods violated protocols trying to profit at others' expenses, he shouldn't complain when the victim eventually outsmarted him. Of course, the victim had better make sure that he could actually outsmart the owner. Things like that had consequences. Not all people endured in silence. Vengeance was common.

The guy haggled with Lobster. He demanded a ransom of two hundred thousand yuan. That was to say, in addition to repaying him for the goods at the parking lot on Caobao Road, Lobster must cover the expenses incurred in getting me and Xiao Mi to this house.

Two hundred thousand yuan was not a very big sum. The problem was that Lobster's hands were full. Remember the line from the movie? You can't grab a gun and money at the same time. Lobster was busy making money, a huge pile of money.

The guy put me on the phone.

I saw her at lunch. Her dress was wrinkled and her hair was a mess. Even so, I liked the way she looked. The guy who had brought me supper the night before ate with us, but all others were gone. He was stout and swarthy, with a weird hairstyle. He was incredibly muscular. A blue vein stood out on his arm whenever he put it to use. He drank liquor from a large bowl. The moment I saw his big tanned hands I knew where we were. He was a fisherman and the house was near the sea. Those hands were used to mooring ropes and fishing nets. If he squeezed the bowl it would crack. Therefore, I'd better not invite trouble even if he was left alone with us.

After lunch Xiao Mi and I were both kept in my room. Maybe they were shorthanded.

She looked much calmer than yesterday. Her only complaint

was she couldn't take showers or change her clothes.

"This is sick. I'm filthy."

"Not at all. I'd be happy to go to bed with you."

"Are you always high?"

"I'm high whenever I see you."

I told her about the phone call to Lobster. She asked, "Do you think Lobster will pay the two hundred thousand yuan?"

I said, "I don't know. It's up to him, not me. It doesn't have much to do with you either."

She regarded me with a strange, I would even say, sympathetic look.

"You never care about anything. If you do, you'd be much more capable than Lobster."

"I only care about you."

"You bother me when you don't care about a thing."

After a while she said, "I don't know, but I like you because you don't have a care in the world."

I comforted her, "Lobster will pay. It's not a big sum. But even if he pays, this thing is not over. You know him."

I rambled on. Whenever the living room outside quieted down, I leaned forward to kiss her. For a while she crossed her legs. I put my hand on her knee, and then I tried to venture under her dress. She stopped me.

"Don't. I feel filthy."

Although I couldn't care less, my hand didn't go further. I just wanted to tease her.

XIV

It almost felt like family living with our kidnappers. During the day we ate together. At night our snore came into a chorus. The atmosphere in this bare solid house would be otherwise perfect if Xiao Mi was in a better mood.

She hated it because there was no shower or change of underwear. The cave-like stone house was humid and smelled of rotten wood. During the day, the wind carried the stink of raw fish into the house. It lingered in rooms and eventually clung to clothes.

Every morning, I was taken to the kitchen to drink tea with the ring leader. Every morning we spoke to Lobster on the phone. Despite Lobster's pleas and threats the ringleader stood his ground. I didn't worry too much. Neither was I terrified. Almost thirty hours had passed since I last saw the fat guy and the thin guy yesterday morning. They were only two people in the gang that terrified me. Physical violence couldn't break me. Once upon a time Lao Cao was cornered in the office by creditors. A dozen knives and even homemade guns were pointed at me. I guarded the door and mediated between them. In the end I shelled out one hundred thousand yuan. Lao Cao was moved to tears of gratitude. When we went out drinking he vowed to return my favor one day.

What terrified me were those guys who didn't understand what knives were for. They didn't have any plan. Some people killed on impulse, others killed according to a plan, and still others killed because they had no idea what to do next. The fat guy and the thin guy belonged to the last category. Luckily they were not here for the moment. Only Jarhead and a few other guys walked about. I had just nicknamed the swarthy guy with the weird hairstyle Jarhead.

Since Jarhead and I were on good terms, I was allowed to loiter in the courtyard. I found a wooden tub under some hanging fishing net in a shed. Judging by the color, the tub was not very ancient. Before presenting it to Xiao Mi, I took it to the kitchen to give it a good scrub and disinfected it with liquor.

I also spotted an old unlocked bicycle in the shed. An idea struck me, but I dismissed it immediately. I didn't know what was out there. Neither did I know where we were. Most importantly, I was quite curious about how the whole kidnapping thing would unfold, not believing for a minute that we would get killed. This was a calculated move of which extreme measures were not a part. This was a bluff to make Lobster cough up the two hundred thousand yuan. He couldn't afford to let his friend down; otherwise his reputation was at risk. Besides, only one of us could escape on the bicycle. I reasoned to myself: if I don't take her away with me, they're still going to demand two hundred thousand yuan, not one hundred thousand yuan.

There were only four people at supper. I talked my head off with Jarhead, pumping him up with all kinds of shit. I told him he could make a fortune selling aquatic produce from here direct to wholesalers in Shanghai. The tricks of the trade I had learned from some wholesaler friends at the Baoshan Pier in Shanghai were very convincing. Then I mentioned sand, which I imagined would abound along the coastline, could also fetch a great price at other places. Excited, he explained the local terrain to me. As a result I knew if I went out of the front entrance, headed south along the path on the other side of the fence, I would reach a fish pier. From the pier a road stretched along the coastline, made a turn at the foot of a hill, and then fed into a highway after a couple of kilometers. Coaches to Fuzhou ran on the highway.

After supper a breeze arose, followed by a rainstorm. Jarhead busied himself replacing door panels and shutting windows. I seized the opportunity to check on Xiao Mi upstairs. Jarhead scrambled to look for me when he found my room empty. Finally, he charged into Xiao Mi's room, shaking his fists at me before grabbing me by the shoulders. I grimaced, hissed, and pleaded innocence. I said it would be more convenient for them to keep us both in the same room. He thought it made some sense, and the intensity in his eyes relaxed. With a solemn face, I suggested that, considering the weather, he keep us in the same room for the night. He rejected it after much hesitation.

Deep in the night typhoon ravaged the house. I dreamed of a gap in the place of my front teeth. I woke up with a start. Xiao Mi was cursing and scurrying barefoot on the wooden floor above me. I rushed into the living room. No one was around. The strong wind and torrential rain covered up my footstep along the creaky stairs. Jarhead didn't make a stir. The light bulb was on in Xiao Mi's room. The dim light danced. The wooden window in the south wall was swung to and fro by the gust. Rainwater flowed on the floorboard near the window. At the sight of me she jumped into the bed and curled up, gesturing towards the window. I ran over to shut the window with force. The horizontal wooden latch across the window pane was too sturdy to be compromised by the wind. It must have been removed on purpose. I said, "Why did you keep the window open against such a gust?"

"I was too upset to sleep. I wish I had just jumped out."

She buried her face on her bent knees, sobbing.

I went over to hug her. She nestled against me and sobbed some more. Her body was ice cold thanks to the strong wind.

She cried, "Lobster dumped me. He doesn't want to pay the two hundred thousand yuan."

I tried to console her, "No way. It's just two hundred thousand. He'll pay without blinking twice."

"No he wouldn't. He hasn't raised the one million yuan yet.

What's more, he may have found out about us."

"How? It's impossible."

"Use your brain. They caught us in the same room."

"Stop speculating." I hugged her, trying to warm her by rubbing her icy cold body with her dress on.

We kissed. I couldn't contain myself on this bizarre night in this treacherous stone house.

"No. No. I stink."

Actions spoke louder than words. I removed her resisting hands from my belly. Not wanting to waste any time taking off her panty, I just pushed it aside.

"You're out of your mind."

"So are you."

"No, I'm not."

"You are. You were just now." I patted her on the ass. "You acted like there was a cramp, down here ..."

"I didn't."

"You did."

"I was just shivering from the cold."

"You'll shiver some more. I'll make you shiver, calm down, and shiver again. On and on."

"You're a bad boy."

For a long while I lost track of the rainstorm outside. Then the noises came back. The wooden panels clanged when the wind went strong and creaked when it weakened. The creaking of our bed was indistinguishable. I felt safe.

She cried again. Her voice was so small and hysterical that it broke my heart. Having stayed in this cave-like stone house in a fishing village by the sea in Southern China for days without a shower in the sultry weather of late summer and early autumn, we smelled like filthy kids. Yes, we were just some innocent kids. Unlike worldly sexual partners, we were not on guard for anyone.

She suddenly looked up at me, her face streaked by tears. In the dim light she told me, "Lobster is not coming. He can't manage it. He has no such money to spare. Run away now. On your own. When you're safe, come back for me."

I looked at her eyes. I saw pleading, command, and sympathy in those eyes. Tears streaks blurred the corners of her mouth into a sneer.

"If you come back for me, I'm yours. Lobster won't care. I'll be all yours."

XV

At dawn I decided to run away. I stood at the door taking one final look at her. She sat in the bed. One leg stretched out, the other curled. The mosquito net cast a shadow on the upper part of her body. I could only make out her disheveled hair and twinkling eyes. The lower part of her body came into view in the dim light. Her dress had been lifted up to the waist. My eyes traced her bare leg from the toes up to the crotch, where the panty hung loosely. After the final look I went downstairs.

I played a trick in my room downstairs. I loosened the steel wire fastening a broomstick, folded it to form two prongs, and then poked them into an electric socket in the wall. Puff, power was out in the entire house.

I jumped out of the window and headed for the shed.

I bent over the bicycle and pedaled desperately against the wind. I saw the pier, where a whole bunch of fishing boats found shelter against the typhoon. Turning right at the small cement square in front of the pier, I was on the road that fed into the highway. The misty sea was to my left. Dawn had not arrived yet. The rain continued. There might be someone pursuing me, but I didn't dare to look back. The wind blew from the sea to push me off the track. I cursed loudly, but the wind drowned it. No one could hear me, not even I myself.

Nobody pursued me. I saw the hill that sloped all the way into the sea. The road swerved drastically at the foot of the hill. Shortly after the turn the highway came into view.

I decided to pedal another half an hour.

Without a watch it was hard to tell how much time had passed by.

I stopped, not sure if I had pedaled long enough. Resting at the doorway of a roadside restaurant, I thumbed a ride from a truck on its way back from delivery. The driver had regarded me suspiciously. I looked like a weirdo riding a bike on a country road in such weather. But eventually he let me sit among a pile of wet manila ropes on the truck bed.

Lobster found me around ten in the morning. When I stood in front of him, he hugged me. He even slapped me on the back. He was imitating mafia bosses in the gangster movies from Hong Kong. I secretly felt embarrassed for him. In my experience, people more likely than not make a fool of themselves when they try to play smart. When they think back, they want a hole to crawl into. Take myself for example. I might have forgotten the major events in my past, but what remained vivid in my memory were often those larger than life postures that filled me with endless remorse.

When I woke up I thought I had slept a long time, but actually it was only a little more than an hour. Lobster must have made many phone calls before waking me up.

We got hold of two vans. I sat in the first one to give directions. It was still raining as we drove on the highway I had come, but in the broad daylight and travelling in the opposite direction it looked different.

"I must be muddled by sleep." I hesitated at each fork. Lobster passed me one cigarette after another. At first, I tried to look for a whitewashed wall. In my vague memory, it was there as soon as I turned into the highway. On its stained surface there were advertisements for seeds and farm tools in blue paint.

Then it occurred to me that that was a tree blown down by the typhoon where the road swerved. My bike almost tripped over it.

In the end, my memory blurred. All hills looked similarly

verdant in the rain. The traffic was pretty heavy on the highway. Vehicles turned off all the time. I was more and more confused.

By three in the afternoon, we finally turned off the right ramp. In less than ten hours, this asphalt road in the shape of a taut bow seemed to have taken on a totally new look. For example, I hadn't noticed that small grocery stall with cases of beer stacked in front of the entrance. At the head of the taut bow, at the foot of the hill that sloped into the sea, there was a house with tall lime gable walls. It might be an ancestral hall. Behind the grove on the sea side of the road was a wide expanse of sand. A disused wooden boat sat solitarily on the white sand.

As our vans approached the cement pier, I saw two women sitting in a small hair salon by the roadside. It was still overcast, although the rain had stopped. There were many people at the pier. Someone shouted at a boat. The fishy odor was much stronger than in the morning. The wind was still blowing from the sea, but it had somewhat subsided. When we made a turn I saw a string of islands in the sea to our southeast. Beyond the islands, the grayish sky and the charcoal gray sea merged on the horizon.

Lobster called the other van to get them ready. Metal clanged in the back seat. The van slowed down. Mud splattered out as tires went over pits. Some pedestrians cast curious glances at our van, but none of them seemed to be wary. At this hour in the afternoon, all was quiet in the fishing village except for the sound of motors running at low speed.

It was reassuring to know that guys in the back seat had withdrawn their knives and there were more knives in the other van. Ten hours had passed since I fled that house. I hoped the rainstorm had prevented Xiao Mi from being moved somewhere else. What's more worrisome was that our opponents might have another plan brewing. They could have mobilized a lot of helpers to the house in the last ten hours. After all, it was Lobster they were interested in, wasn't it? If that was the case we would have a bigger headache.

In that case an open fight would break out. You could hardly foresee the outcome when you played against a home team.

Before leaving the hotel I had mentioned this possibility to Lobster. But he was a man of action. I mean, if he was at a duel like those depicted in movies, he would most likely be the first one to shoot. A born daredevil, he believed in first-mover advantages.

Not surprisingly, he just laughed at my caution and shoved me into the van. If I were him I'd rather pay the two hundred thousand yuan. It was the best to settle money disputes with money. That was my philosophy.

Both vans staggered at slow speed for several hundred meters on the rugged road. All of a sudden, Lobster barked into the phone, "Now!"

Both vans accelerated abruptly, knocking down the fence at over eighty miles per hour. No sooner had they parked on the muddy peanut patch than doors slid open. Men with knives leapt off, crashed into the front entrance, and searched the house: bedrooms, the kitchen, the toilet. Three of them went upstairs.

There was no one.

XVI

I sank into deep sleep in the hotel room. When I woke up it was already ten at night. The TV flickered in the dark room. Shadows danced on the ceiling. Chaotic scenes flashed by on TV. Some helmeted soldiers were hiding behind an armored vehicle. A guy was pointing at a building. The volume was turned down. The voiceover seemed to report arrests made at the Parliament Building in Moscow. I turned my head and found Lobster smoking by the coffee table. Behind him a window was wide open. Outside the window dark clouds had dispersed. A gentle wind came in. The cigarette in Lobster's hand burned brighter. He was looking at me.

I explained to him, "Those soldiers are sharp. They are from the Dzerzhinskiy Division. They are charged with the task of garrisoning the Soviet capital. They fought in the Battle of Moscow in WWII. Have you seen that bullshit movie? Later, the division merged into the KGB. They guarded Comrade Lenin's coffin."

"You know a lot."

"I'm just talking nonsense. Their grandpas guarded Lenin's coffin."

"You really know a lot."

"It's not always a good thing."

"What you know slows you down."

"You are not that slow."

"I'm much slower than you are. If someone with a gun

charges into this room now, you'd be gone before I realize it. You may jump out of the window. You may hide in the bathroom. That's why you can't afford to know too much."

I knew about his past. He had often confided in me after drinking more than a half bottle of Chivas Regal. Once, at ten years of age to be exact, he was cast away by two competing gangs. He had learned a lot from street life.

I had seen it with my own eyes. Once I was talking to him as we came out of an elevator. In a split second he was gone. What I mean is, before you react, before I weigh all eleven alternatives and finally decide on one, Lobster has already found the easiest way out.

I switched on the light and lit a cigarette. Since I hadn't slept well or long enough, I felt hot and stuffy despite the breezes. But they were more pressing matters than sleep, so I fetched a can of coke from the refrigerator. After a huge gulp and a loud belch, my mind cleared up.

I was waiting for him to bring the matter up, although I had a pretty good idea what he was going to say. Last night, Xiao Mi had said Lobster couldn't afford the two hundred thousand yuan. It had sounded weird at the moment, because two hundred thousand wasn't a big sum. However, I had been distracted. On our way back earlier this evening, I had time to think it over.

The attack during the day was intended to build up pressure on the other party, but at the end of the day you had to make some concession. It was clever of them to demand two hundred thousand yuan, a sum that was neither small nor astronomical. You'd lose face if you couldn't pay. Of course there was another solution possible. If you knew enough people, you could build up the pressure further, until the other party buckle and send Xiao Mi back. For sure, they would not send Xiao Mi back directly. Instead they would find a reputable mediator who was on good terms with both sides. The mediator would invite both sides to a banquet, and then Xiao Mi would come back. In that case your face would be saved. You would even be held in higher regard than if you paid the ransom. However, such an approach still cost a lot of money, probably more than two hundred thousand yuan. In certain circumstances it could develop into a gamble, just like what happened in a game of Show Hand. If you wanted the other player to show you more cards, you must place more wagers. In the end the wagers were so high that either you or the other player would be maxed out.

Gang wars didn't help in the aspect. I'm serious. Competing gangs did resort to "wars", on which many stories circulated. Once upon a time, a guy chartered a plane in order to bring about a hundred people down to Guangzhou to seek revenge. Such practices didn't put an end to disputes, though. It would cost you all your money in the end.

"How did you seduce my chick? She has a high opinion of you. I caught her ogling you a lot."

"You know a lot too, even her ogles."

She didn't usually ogle men. Instead she sat still looking at nobody. But she always knew if a man checked her out. There were women like that in this world. Of course there are also those other women who kept ogling you if they wanted to sleep with you.

"I read books too, although not as many as you do. I would never stay in a seven hundred or eight hundred yuan hotel room just to read a novel. But I read too."

He was right. Not only did he read, but he memorized as well. Lobster had a photographic memory. I'm not saying I had a faulty memory, but my attention was diverted because I tended to read between lines. As a result he remembered more things from books.

"This time you have to go all out." He waved his hand as if driving away a mosquito. Since the room was on a top floor, mosquitoes were unlikely to get in from the open window. So this was more likely a gesture of resolution. "You've never focused before. But this is a rare opportunity. If you seize it, you'll make big money."

I saw what he meant. He was good at forestalling his opponent by a show of strength. He placed big bets when he actually held a disappointing hand of cards. This tactics was called bluffing in books. I must think it over.

Lao Cao would yield if I stood my ground. Some comprise could be reached. The favor I did for him and my track record were an asset. Timing was important. If necessary I could use some tricks. I could manage it if I had enough control.

Lao Cao always demanded collateral. If you wanted to borrow 1 million from him, you must keep at least one and half million's worth of goods in his warehouse. You could ask your buyer to make payment and take delivery right there. In that case you could use part of the money that had just come in to repay Lao Cao, principal plus interest, and your buyer could leave with the goods.

One term in the tentative deal was in Lobster's favor: the owner of goods only demanded an advance of one million yuan, not the full amount. Once the advance was made, in theory Lobster could ask for as many deliveries as he could before accounts were settled in three months' time. The key problem was we didn't have the one million to be paid into the owner's bank account in Fuzhou. With the unexpected kidnap we needed one million two hundred thousand in total. Without any collateral we couldn't borrow from Lao Cao. Without the one million the owner of goods wouldn't deliver to us.

A business-as-usual arrangement with Lao Cao was impossible. He was too cautious to make a loan that went unpledged for a minimum of three days. Moreover, even if he extended the loan to us, God knew what might happen before the cargo ship reached a port.

After the typhoon came the clear night sky. With a couple of hours' sleep and two more cans of chilled coke, my brain worked pretty well. The two empty cans were still sweating on the night table. In ten minutes the two of us worked out a perfect plan.

XVII

I called Lü Yan on a pay phone at the airport to have him get me a new cell phone using my old number. The thin guy took my Nokia phone. I had a good appetite at Café de Coral on Beijing Road, where I finished a plate of blood clams, a glass bowl of liquor-soaked shrimps, and two bottles of beer. After the meal I took a taxi to Hotel Equatorial, planning to kill the next two hours on a bowling lane there. Someone said hello when I was changing into bowling shoes.

The guy had a deathly pale face and a bang over the corner of his eyes. He acted familiar, but I couldn't recall who he was. The woman with him smiled at me. She reminded me of having met the guy somewhere.

The guy was wearing a black V-neck T-shirt. His thin white jeans wrapped around his ass tightly and the crotch area bulged. They reminded me of an air compressor and a drill. They must keep the woman high all the time. The idea soon got hold of me. A spot inside my head, probably between two eyes, was triggered and a signal was sent to my hands, urging them to punch the guy in the belly or to smash him with my shoes. However, what sanity was left kept me from doing so. I knocked the rubber sole of my Bally shoe on the metal edge of the bowling lane instead.

He claimed that we had sat next to each other at a dinner party. Since there were two hours to go before my 10 p.m. appointment, I agreed readily to bet on a game of bowling or two.

"A grand for the winner?"

That was the wrong thing to say. If you seek a heart-throbbing night, name a larger bet to get yourself stimulated. If you just want to kill two hours, limit the wager to how much you have with you. In the latter case, just mention it casually when you select balls. An earnest suggestion like that only proves you a rookie.

I countered by proposing three games and five hundred bucks for each.

I played pretty well, with strikes in two consecutive frames. Sometimes I acted inferior just to lure him to up the ante. It was neither necessary nor worthwhile, but I wanted to enjoy myself. I threw a series of curve balls, but he just bowled the balls straight down the lane. I was almost depressed. Was it really entertaining for a person with a full stomach to throw straight balls frame after frame? I lost two games in the end.

I paid him without accepting his invitation to the bar. You can play bowling with a guy you don't like, but never drink with him.

I left Hotel Equatorial for Hilton Hotel. On the corner of Yan'an Road and Huashan Road, the well-lit office of Korean Air was deserted. The bluish white fluorescent light was at odds with the air of debauchery oozing from the surrounding hotels. Just imagine how a one-night-stand couple would look in the fluorescent light as they emerged from a hotel, their feet limb from exhaustion, their faces flushed and their smiles disoriented. Dim streetlights and tree shadows would work much better.

I had been going over the matter again and again since boarding the plane in Fuzhou. Last night I was too worn out to think straight. After catching up on sleep I looked at the matter from a different perspective. Lobster had tried in vain to reach the kidnappers since we stormed the house. He asked around while I booked us tickets for the 5 p.m. flight back to Shanghai.

Lobster had called when I was at Café de Coral saying Lao

Chen had struck a deal on behalf of us with the kidnappers. Now I must act.

It was wrong to confuse the two hundred thousand ransom with the 1 million advance payment. I came to the realization after catching up on sleep. Lobster had taken advantage of me.

All this was for a woman who had cried in front of me in a solitary stone house on a stormy night, sweat stuck to her skin and the smell from her dress triggering one's tender feelings. It was all these details, the smell, the tears, and the wrinkled dress, that had made me lose my head. You can't afford to lose your head in our circle. You must chew on the remarks made by others to pick up clues.

Once you have chewed on the remarks made by others, the turning point in an event would be as plain as day. You won't delay your decision to the next minute. Have you played that game when you were little? You stand facing the wall. A row of your playmates stand a dozen meters away from you. You slap the wall continuously and turn your head around every few random seconds. Your playmates sneak closer to you from the line you've drawn on the ground with a brick. But they do it while you are facing the wall. If you turn around and catch a guy moving, he is out. If someone manages to approach you and pat you on the shoulder, you lose.

That's what I mean by the turning point in an event. In the game, you must catch fellow players who had approached you but had yet to reach your shoulder. Where they stood right now was irrelevant. Focus on the split second when they were ready to pounce. You could take history as a mirror. Xiang Yu failed to capture Liu Bang at the banquet although he had many opportunities to do so[1], from the moment Liu Bang came in to the time he raised his wine cup for the first toast, until the sword dance performed by two dumb underlings. He could

---

1   Xiang Yu and Liu Bang were two prominent leaders of insurgent forces who rebelled against the Qin Dynasty from 209 BC to 206 BC.—*Trans.*

have captured Liu Bang and killed him. The fight for the throne would be over. However, Xiang Yu failed to seize any of those split seconds.

However, the die had been cast. Last night, instead of challenging Lobster, I had contributed quite some ideas as to how to reassure Lao Cao. I said we could ask Lao Cao to send a man of his own to keep an eye on us in Fuzhou. I had stood in Lobster's shoes and lost my neutrality just because I wanted to show off how smart I was.

I didn't do it just for a woman. The draught induced by the two high-rise hotels facing each other, Hilton Hotel and Hotel Equatorial, sobered me up. I shouldn't blame it all on a woman. It was because of me, a smart ass who believed that one could get away from all vortexes beneath the smooth surface of the river of life like an agile fish.

I sat on a sofa by the window in the thirty-ninth floor bar of Hilton Hotel. There was a vertical distance of about one hundred meters between me and Huashan Road to my left. After half a glass of Chivas Regal my body seemed to float in the dark midair. I looked down through the window constantly. Streetlights and tree shade cast shadows of motley shapes on the ground. Cars swooshed by. My legs were a bit limp at first, but soon the vertigo was replaced by soothing giddiness.

I had asked Lü Yan to drive Lao Cao over for urgent business. Lao Cao was never a night animal, but he would venture out if you offered him a ride. Lao Cao was a role model of dedication for hustlers. He injected fresh air into our circle. He played his cards cautiously and conscientiously when all other gamblers prayed for a flush. He was proof that men were born with certain qualities. A man could go astray, but wherever he goes, he was either a hustler or not.

XVIII

"No urgent business is good business." No sooner had they sat down than I asked Lao Cao for a loan of one million two hundred thousand. If you're not sure about something, bring it up as soon as possible.

"This is good business. A loan of one month at five percent. I will keep cell phones in your warehouse as collateral. Five hundred units."

"Cell phones? Who can I sell to if you default?"

There was a stage in the other end of the bar. It was neither spacious nor cramped. Half of the stage was taken up by stereos and keyboards. The other half was roomy enough for the Southeast Asian singer to swing her breasts. The height of the stage was deliberate. You'd think you could see her legs when seated, but when if you really sat down you saw nothing. Lü Yan simply brought his glass to a table close to those legs.

"Five hundred units for one million two hundred thousand. You have to pay one million and a half million for them if they're delivered on international waters. The unit price is low enough for you to sell out at one go in Zhongguancun[1] in Beijing."

"I want two hundred more units."

I had yet to play my trump card, but there was no hurry. Let the prospects of making sixty thousand yuan out of one loan

---

1 Zhongguancun is known as China's Sillicon Valley. The electronics marketplaces there are also famous.—*Trans.*

sink in first. Life is hard for a loan shark. If any debtor defaults, he has to coin his brain to sell the collateral. Sometimes he lends out money and gets back a big headache. To cure the headache he has to spend more money, a lot of money. The sixty thousand yuan could help pay rent on his warehouse and office as well as salary for his employees.

Maybe I could wait until tomorrow morning to play the trump card in his office. After one night's consideration, he would be inclined to agree. Then I would play the trump card. He would found the deal harder to resist, and I would be able to bluff it out. In such circumstances it would be easier for him to say yes than no. After all, it was just a slight deviation from his usual practice. As long as he sent a trustworthy man of his own to go to Fuzhou with us, he would have everything under control. Of course, in the end it was me who had everything under control. I was certainly trustworthy, although he and I might have different definitions for the word "trustworthy".

Lao Cao's new wife was more than twenty years his junior. When I saw her last time, she was wearing a corduroy maternity overall. I believe her pregnancy had a lot to do with Lao Cao's rigorous approach to loan sharking among hustlers. Loan sharking was a bad trade in itself. It was funny to stick to rules among rule breakers. However, I admired him. He handled money for gamblers, but he never gambled himself. This required self-perception as well as a cool head. A man must know what he wants.

After I lit the third cigarette, Lao Cao shook his head and tried to dispel the rings of smoke with his hand. He became restless. Eventually he stood up to go to the bathroom. Maybe he wanted to find fresh air there. Lü Yan moved back. "A lot of people came for Lobster at our Yandang Road apartment."

"The same cops?"

"And some other cops," he said. "And other people. Cops and Robbers. Robbers and cops. What a scene!"

"He has made quite a number of acquaintances."

"True."

Alcohol turned Lü Yan into a chatterbox. Two ounces of Chival Regal was enough to flap his tongue as rapidly as an electronic toy bird flapped its wings.

"One million and two hundred thousand. What a strange amount! I mean, why not round it up? They calculate down to the last digit for the advance payment."

Should I congratulate him on his astuteness? No. I just shook my head. Unlike him, I grew quieter as I drank more.

Around 11 p.m. we descended to ground level. The elevator sped down. I was a bit giddy. Maybe it was because of the alcohol.

We stood in the vestibule waiting for Lü Yan to drive the car over. It was a night serene enough for honest people to have a sound sleep. I read somewhere that all people who got up at six in the evening were honest. Well put. As for those people who still loitered around in streets, such a night was fair enough. At least those barelegged chicks wouldn't freeze when they came out of bars.

"It's a different age." Lao Cao looked out of the car window crouching in the front seat. Bamboo scaffoldings were erected around a building. The retrofit project was halfway through, and the new look was almost there. I could see a huge triangular roof and lots of cement columns. Someone who had come into a big sum of money wanted to make it over into a shoddy money squandering den: ball room on the ground floor, karaoke bar on the second, private rooms on upper floors staffed with girls in ill-fit cheongsams. A competent madam would make sure they all had long legs. A competent operator could convert a floor or two into rooms for clients to play poker, sleep or do something else.

"They crop up everywhere." Money was all what Lao Cao thought about between sleep and meals. "They say it's quick money. The other day a guy showed me a proposal. With sixty private rooms the payback period was only eighteen months."

"It's no easy money at all. You worry a lot." I sat further away from the window. Lao Cao had rolled down the front window. It felt chilly on the back seat.

"Much easier than what you do."

I believed otherwise. There is a difference between being wicked only when conditions were right and being wicked all the time. In my opinion, it was generally a good idea; I would even say an elegant act, to play a wicked trick on a carefully chosen target that had evil intentions himself. However, if you play wicked trick all the time and on everyone, you would disdain yourself and develop a bad mood.

"I heard Lobster was in this line of business too."

This didn't sound like Lobster. Although Lü Yan claimed he had heard about it too, I was dubious. This was most likely some tale spun at a dinner party. Why would Lobster get into such a business? If you had a place like that, you had to report to work on time and put on a smile every day. You had to deal with uniformed government agents and scums with or without knives. You had to haggle with wine dealers, make rounds, worry about peeled wall paper, a bartender who poured two extra ounces for his friends and prostitutes who fought over patrons.

You must have high taste even if you're a hustler, right? You can't just chase money. For me, money is not the most important. Money is important, but not the most important. I mean, when you saunter into the Shanghai Jinjiang Dickson Center and take a fancy to a Japanese trench coat with a price label of over seven thousand yuan, money is important. However, that is just a reward for you. After bluffing a poker player holding two Aces with two Kings into submission, of course you should reward yourself. Nevertheless, what made your heart race during the game while keeping your countenance was not the reward, but the teetering sense of walking a tightrope. You caught your breath, because in the next moment you may fall or you may win standing ovation, right?

XIX

In our circle, only a guy who had barely survived a flop rented an office at a cheap location. As soon as he made a bit of money from some deals he would move his office to a more decent address, such as that of a school, a research institute, or an association whose mission remained mysterious to outsiders. These organizations had a lot of vacant rooms for lease at reasonable prices. If he made a fortune he would become a tenant at one of those office complexes that had sprung up everywhere in recent years. Such an office usually came with huge shuttered windows, walls painted in grayish white, and synthetic carpet. With some plywood executive desks, a few imitation leather executive chairs, a glass coffee table, two phones, and a fax machine, his business was launched into a new phase. If this hustler had a taste as good as the three of us, he could also rent space in a commercial-residential complex.

Lao Cao leased a small decrepit factory on North Caoxi Road. I looked for the narrow alley as soon as the car passed Jianguo Hotel. It always took me efforts to spot the turn into the obscure alley barely one hundred meters long. His factory stood at the end. All workshops had been converted into warehouses. The mosaic tiles mounted on the façade of the small administrative building reminded me of public toilets. It was eight-thirty in the morning. I yelled out Lao Cao's name. He poked his head out of the aluminum alloy window of a second-floor office and beckoned me up. None of his a dozen employees had shown up yet.

His office looked modest. However, upon further scrutiny you would realize it was actually sound proof and air tight. That aroused suspicion. Of course, if your hustler friends hung out here discussing all kinds of outlandish businesses, caution was necessary. You couldn't afford to let your employees in the outer office answering phones get wind of anything, could you?

He seemed to have bought all furniture in this office second-hand. I sat on the small sofa, resting my feet on a steel folding chair. Tealeaves uncurled in the glass, yawns became irresistible. When I shook my legs, either the sofa of the chair creaked. I told him, "I want the money today."

"Shall I remind you that this is a loan, not debt?"

The office was clean and bright. The floor was wet from recent mopping. The blind were drawn up to let in sunshine and morning breeze. This was indeed an office full of positive energy. Despite its shady function, it looked much more decent than our apartment on Yandang Road, where you woke up in the morning and stumbled into a living room littered with empty beer cans and stinky glass. Women's clothes were strewn dubiously over the huge genuine leather sofa, my favorite piece of furniture provided by our landlord. At the apartment on Yandang Road, what you saw after getting up would lure you into bed or make you pop open a can of coke and doze the morning off on a high-back chair.

In such an office filled with fine sunshine and humidity from evaporating dew on foliage, a person would set his mind on doing something for his wife and children, if not for world peace. On such an exhilarating morning and in such an upbeat office, I put on a confident smile in order to trap my old friend sitting at the desk by the window, the old friend who would more likely than not accommodate me for some favor owed in the past. Having just mopped the floor, he was fully contented and mindful of his young wife who was carrying his baby.

"You want the money today? What about the collateral?"

I rubbed my eyes and yawned. This was key. I'd better pause to let him feel my hesitation, or maybe he would interpret it as a kind of apology. A sparrow perched on the stainless steel burglary-resistant window mesh. There was the smell of burning wood in the air. Many residents in this part of suburban Shanghai were still using firewood stoves. A brick chimney rose to the southeast of the window about fifty meters away—the range of an air rifle if you fancied sparrow shooting. A wisp of white smoke drifted out of the blackish chimney whose top was about the height of our window.

The established practice of Lao Cao was for borrowers to deposit collaterals in his warehouse, which was the row of old factory buildings in the yard visible from this window. There was a gap between the roof and the walls of each decrepit frame structure building. In the past, when the factory had had enough orders to keep running, the gap let in sufficient light. But now it was boarded up with rotten planks. The windows in the walls were sealed up with angle irons as well.

"You can't keep my goods here," I told him. "This piece of shit place isn't right for cell phones. You must keep them in the office. No damp is allowed."

"All right."

"Give me two hundred thousand in cash and one million in a money order."

Lao Cao had owed me a favor. Back then he had had such a hard time that all the IOU notes he wrote out could be pieced together to make a pair of short pants. I helped him because I didn't believe he was truly down and out. Now that he was on his feet again, it was time for me to ask him to return the favor, although the way I asked was not chummy enough, at least in details. Anyway, the modifications to his established practices couldn't go as far as to cause calamities.

"Goods will be delivered in Fuzhou. The first batch has to be delivered there. So—"

"The loan is impossible."

"It's still possible. There is a way."

Lao Cao fished out a ball of newspaper from under his desk

to scrub one of the steel bars that made up the burglary-resistant mesh.

"Bird dropping." He shot the ball into the waste paper basket in the corner.

"Give the money order to a man you trust and make him travel to Fuzhou with me."

"That is extraordinary. You guys have lots of tricks up your sleeves."

"You can always count on me. Your man keeps the money order. Once he sees the goods loaded, he calls you, and you tell him to hand over the money order to me. You arrange for trucks. I'll pay for the transportation. Once the goods are in your trucks, they are yours."

"Nope. You guys come up with new tricks all the time. I'm not sophisticated enough to play with you."

"He only takes orders from you. No handover until after delivery."

The smell of burning wood in the air was gone. Someone unlocked the office next door, entered, and dragged a chair. Lao Cao went over to close our door, came back, and took his seat again.

"Can you swear this is a simple deal?" He stared at me, his made-in-Japan gilt spectacle frame glistening in the morning sun. He was all sincerity, as if begging me to tell the truth.

"Nothing can be simpler. All cards are on the table."

I felt I was telling the truth. It was a simple deal, except that Lobster must pay the Taiwanese before taking delivery, which he could then resell for much more money. Anyway, as far as Lao Cao was concerned, this was a simple deal.

The phone rang. He answered. As he hung up he said, "OK. Just for this one time."

I took out a cigarette, but the lighter was nowhere to be found. So I lit it with a match from a matchbox on the lower shelf of the glass coffee table. He was still talking: "I will give you two hundred thousand in cash. If you screw it, I'll deduct it from your account."

XX

After a shower and a shave, I called Lao Xu's room.

I hadn't had an idle moment. The day before, I had sat in Lao Cao's office until I got the two hundred thousand yuan in cash in the evening. He had written a check payable to a restaurant, and the restaurant was supposed to provide the cash, which was about its two-day business turnover. In the meanwhile I attended to many other matters, including booking two plane tickets at a ticket office and having a threesome lunch at the Ten Ten Seafood Harbor in Xujiahui. The best way to observe a person is to eat with him, right?

At about ten in the morning, Lao Cao summoned a Mr. Xu to his office by a house phone. He was a money manager under Lao Cao and he was going to Fuzhou with me. Like Lao Cao, Lao Xu was in his forties. God must have made both of them with the same mold. They belonged to the type of people who wore galoshes when the sky was just overcast. In my opinion, Lao Cao still took occasional risks. If his feet were well protected, he would poke his bare head into the rain now and then. As for Lao Xu's risk appetite, I didn't care that much. What mattered was his memory. A person who spent his day keeping books and reconciling accounts must have a decent memory, right?

Over lunch I pulled out my phone. "Shit," I said. "I've forgotten the number. Lao Xu, do you remember the number of the hotel in Fuzhou I wrote on a slip of paper and handed to you together with the plane ticket? Remember, I told you to call

Lobster to let him know our arrival time in Fuzhou?" "Back then I was in a hurry to leave, but nobody answered my many phone calls. Lobster must be somewhere else." Of course Lobster was somewhere else, because instead of his room extension I wrote the one of the room next door, which I had paid for an extra week before leaving Fuzhou. But Lao Xu had no idea. So he dialed many times. "Do you still remember the number?"

He only remembered part of it. He was right about the general number. As for the extension, he was wrong in one digit the first time, two digits the second time, and all four digits the third try.

After lunch we went to the bank to get the money order. When the bank teller handed it to Lao Cao, I was by his side. I took it over and studied it carefully. Lao Cao said, "What? You haven't seen that amount of money before?"

This morning, I made a second trip to the bank, where I deposited the two hundred thousand yuan cash into a credit card for Lobster to withdraw in Fuzhou. In addition to a phone call to Lobster to inform him of the deposit, I also faxed him a sheet of paper. It took me quite some efforts to create the content on the sheet the night before.

This afternoon, the security guard at the Hongqiao Airport eyed me suspiciously before poring over my ID. Only then did I realize that I hadn't shaven. I finished the last pages of the detective story during the flight, turning a blind eye and a deaf ear to a Lao Xu who either wriggled in his seat to look at the gilt-edged clouds or blabbered at me. An inexperienced traveler was excitable. I would let the excitement build up. When the shrewd lawyer who liked to imagine himself a knight saved the wronged pretty woman with a compelling defense in court, the MacDonell-Douglass plane we flew in was banking and descending. The ground rose up directly to the cabin. Lao Xu was so jittered that he shut the window shade abruptly.

By seven in the evening we were in downtown Fuzhou. I took Lao Xu to the Overseas Chinese Hotel. Lobster was out.

He was most probably experiencing in person the dangerous situation one usually saw in movies: two gangs ate at the same table. They all carried weapons. There was a mediator. In a bag on the table laid the two hundred thousand yuan cash wrapped in newspaper in one or two stacks. Everyone was tense. A fight might break out any time. The veteran fighters among them were able to stab a stiletto into a body without moving a muscle of the countenance. The stab would be about one centimeter below the shoulder and the distance of the width of the stiletto above the heart. The forceful thrust would cause the victim crash to the floor. Everybody else would be awed. However, despite the ugly look the wound was not lethal. The perpetrator remained in his seat as if he had done nothing except a graceful gesture that sent a knife into the hollow part of a person's shoulder.

Certainly, these things didn't happen if the mediator was well respected. Usually the two sides would make peace after a few friendly drinks, the side that got the worse of the deal looking forward to a next time and the side that profited from the deal determined to take precautions. When Lobster pushed the money to the other side, their leader would call some guys somewhere in the city to let the hostage walk. The plot was no different from that in movies, which was not surprising at all. If you hung out in an enclosed circle, you were bound to act. The good thing about hanging out in such a circle was that you had a single objective and therefore a simpler life devoid of any sense of helplessness or sentimentality. Yet it did come with a downside, i.e., events might turn out to be too dramatic.

The restaurant was deserted. We sat all alone at a huge round table right below the tinkling and jingling chandelier. Waiters busied around us. Lao Xu went after the snowy white razor clams. I had no appetite. For one thing, my eardrums were still ringing. For another, I was obsessively preoccupied with doubts about my own memory. I was exhausted. I must have a good sleep.

But this was no time to sleep. I had to check Lao Xu into the hotel. "Give me your ID. I'll take care of the checking in. Enjoy the beer, but don't drink too much. They say beer plus seafood equals poison." I dropped my head and dragged my feet out of the restaurant. After making my way through the labyrinthine corridors I stood in line at the reception desk behind a young girl. She was carrying a huge backpack and a rolling suitcase stood by her. Why do you have to wear that hat? I'll bet you're from either Beijing or Taiwan, because people in both places have a penchant for hats. Your hat looks like a flattened beer can. How weird! A receptionist was attending to her now. "The floor you request has sold out, but rooms are available on any other floor." Before going back to the restaurant, I had one more errand to run, a trip to the hotel business center.

After having the receptionist send a VCR to Lao Xu's room, I called him to wish him a good night.

It was not yet eight o'clock in the evening, but I went to bed anyway. The room smelled of cheap air freshener. I didn't want to get up to open the window. I had just drawn the gauze curtain, but not the thick velvet curtain, because I didn't like sleeping in a dark place. I buried my head in the pillow, although it didn't help much. Both the pillow case and the sheets smelled of bleach, but at least that was a much cleaner smell. I didn't dwell on the complicated game moves. Let them wait till another day. Now, in the humming of the air conditioner and between cool clean sheets, I wanted some simple thoughts to lull myself to sleep. I was going to see her tomorrow. By then she should have bathed and her hair would have a mint scent. But the sight of her would remind me of her smell on that typhoon night. That night, the smell permeated my nose, my hands and my shirt. And it stayed the next day. Lobster must have sensed it because I spent the entire afternoon with him in the same van. The smell must be a revelation to him, without him realizing it. Smells were mysterious messengers.

At that time I was leaning against the van door and looking out. I briefed him again on the layout inside the house.

"… I sneaked upstairs. Everything creaked and clanged in the typhoon. Nobody could hear me …" I told him in detail how I had escaped. I could have left this part out. Why did I tell him? There was a long unaccounted for interval between the time I went up and the time I left the house. What did I try to indicate by my half-hearted honesty? He just looked out of the window at the cloudy sky and the rolling green fields. He lit a cigarette. "How weird! They let you move about."

By far I had gained a slight upper hand. She had put cards into my hand and now I was playing them. I had laid down a huge stake with a view of winning. Actually the stake was financed by someone else, but anyway I didn't cower. Now the cards were on the table. So was the stake. It was her turn. By far I had gained a slight upper hand. As for Lobster, it was too early to worry about him. He knew how to make his choice. As for me, nothing really mattered. I didn't play the game because of what she had said to me. On that typhoon night, she told me, "If you come back for me, I'm yours." Such a sentence was after all irrelevant. It was natural for a woman in her circumstances to say so. If you shut a woman up in a stone house that stank of rotten fish and shrimp for days without giving her access to showers and clean clothes, she would go crazy and say things without thinking. I didn't do this just because of what she had said. I was not that susceptible. For a moment I was carried away with her smell, not a pleasant smell at that. However, if you were kept in a stinky house for days, such a smell would be refreshing. It was the smell of a mixture of ice cold tears and sweaty flesh, not that of mint or lemon (common fragrance among those other women). I was indeed sensitive to smells. That long-winded French guy was right, smells were associated with memory. I didn't mean the smell of a cake. That was another matter entirely. What I meant was you remembered the smell of a person many years later even if her face had become vague.

The problem was you couldn't cower when it was your turn to play a hand. Right? If it was your turn, you must play.

Sometimes, what mattered was neither the outcome nor the stake, but whether you played your card or not. I was seized with a fit of worry. So I recited the serial number silently again. I suspected myself of obsessive compulsive disorder. To dispel these thoughts I told myself repeatedly not to think about the serial number. "Don't think about it. You've memorized it the first time. Get some sleep." The serial number fleeted across the screen in my mind ceaselessly. By and by I fell asleep.

XXI

"They didn't realize you were gone until the morning." I smoked in bed while Xiao Mi spoke from the sofa. "Around seven o'clock, a van took me away to Fuzhou, I guess. There were three people in addition to the two we knew."

It was another morning. Lobster was sitting on a sofa by the window, his legs crossed, his eyes concentrated on the cigarette in his hand. Between him and Xiao Mi was a coffee table. On the coffee table there was a thermal flask, some glass, and a glass ashtray. Xiao Mi sat on the smaller sofa to its right. Her legs were visible by my nightstand, left on right, with a bulge on her calf.

"… I was taken to the sixth floor of a house. Two men guarded me. I spent a whole day there. By night time they took me out and drove around. Then they dumped me in a street."

I was not particularly interested in her story. I didn't raise one million two hundred thousand million for that. If there were only the two of us, I would have asked her some other questions. But I would take my time and set priorities right. First of all, I asked Lobster whether he had had the stuff made. He put out his cigarette. Of course it was being made. I demanded to see it with my own eyes. This was going to be a memory trick. Memory is enigmatic. If you are sure about your own memory, then you assume others ignore things you go out of your way to memorize. In the current circumstance, it mattered enormously if others indeed ignored things you wanted them to ignore.

However, you will never know for sure what others remember and what else they forget. For example, you are sitting in an obscure corner of a hotel lobby waiting for somebody when some stranger approaches you raving about a party two years ago. You are unable to recall a thing. Doesn't it prove that others—people you feel superior to—sometimes have better memory than you do? Memory is mysterious. It is triggered by more than smells, although smells may sometimes help you recall. Nevertheless, smells were not crucial to the matter at hand.

"It'll be available tomorrow afternoon," Lobster informed me.

"Then show me tomorrow."

"Sure. Tomorrow."

I was on a path of no return, no longer neutral as a friend or prudent enough as a businessman. I could have taken a solid stand, but the kidnap cut the ground from under my feet. I was in. Discussions, negotiations, rejections, and reluctant agreements were out of the question. Therefore, from now on I must watch each step and take matters into my own hands, no details spared. The problem was—

"Lao Xu must have some fun while he is in Fuzhou. You take care of it."

"I'll find him a chick. Consider it done." Why was he so matter-of-fact when talking about women? Lü Yan would be different. Lü Yan would certainly utter the same sentence with a lewd smile.

Pigeons swept past the window. The gauze curtain billowed in the breeze. Xiao Mi laughed as if choked, or you could say she laughed to get your attention. She was shaking all over without making much noise, which reminded me of her shaking the other time.

Seconds later, Lobster turned to her. "Why do you laugh?"

She went on laughing her unrestrained laughter as if she had gone crazy.

"Nothing. A thought just popped into my mind," she told Lobster. "Are his hands really that capable? Can he really perform that trick in public?"

I looked into her eyes until she stopped laughing. Then I leapt out of bed, fished out a pack of cards from the nightstand drawer, pushed the ashtray and telephone aside. First, I showed her the cards in my palms. They were two kings. Then I put my palms together. When I showed her my palms again, the two kings had become two queens. After another go, the two kings reappeared.

"He has some tricks up his sleeves. Many girls fell for them in the past," Lobster said.

There was a slight trace of sarcasm in her eyes. She said, "It's no big deal. He's just got bigger hands."

"Would you like to try?"

"Easy. Tell me how and give me some time to practice. I'll show you tomorrow."

Both Lobster and I burst out laughing. He was louder.

"Don't you believe me? Women have smaller but more dexterous hands."

Was that her joke? Was it how women tell jokes? It was indeed impressively dexterous. She made two men laugh, but one of them had no clue why the other laughed, therefore becoming part of the joke. How long does it take to learn to tell such riddle-like jokes? How long does it take for women to master such tricks? A thousand years? Ten thousand years? Now, I wanted to be more honest. I liked her joke, and I liked the sarcasm in her eyes, although maybe it was just because I understood what she was implying, or because I wasn't part of the joke this time.

"But it is Friday tomorrow. Banks are closed the day after tomorrow," I said.

"We can wait until next week to pay and take delivery."

Now I felt a little better than a moment ago. Some doubts had lifted. I deserved the torment wherein one hundred thoughts contradicted another one hundred thoughts. I deserved the fate of those novelists who turned one or two illusory motives in their minds into full-length fiction, who turned fantasy into reality. The world doesn't run that way. What is real is real, what is fictitious should remain fictitious. If you endeavor to ground illusion in reality, if you consider such endeavor an adventure game, then you deserve the torment of which doubts are the least severe. You'll learn later.

The sun poured in from the window behind them onto the floorboard by my bed. The dirt on the tip of my Bally shoes was more visible than ever, the dirt that had stuck and dried up since the night of typhoon. It was inadequate vestige to prove that something had happened that night, but it at least made the illusion more solid.

Lobster was on the phone.

"You must get it done this afternoon … no … nope … I'll pay extra to get it done this afternoon … OK, see you at two."

He put down the phone and headed for the bathroom. I left the bed to pour some water from the thermal flask on the nightstand into a glass. As I bent I could see the sun shine on her right cheek as well as the hollow between her neck and shoulder. She assumed an upright posture, her head turned the other way on purpose to look intently at the corner formed by the nightstand and the wall as if an enthralling show was being staged there. However, her blouse had slipped slightly down her right shoulder, which was quite tempting since I stood very close. For a second or two, I had an urge to do something, like kissing her on that hollow, or brushing a finger across the area under her collarbone where her breast was about to rise, the area that hid in the shadow between her undone first button and a clasped second button. However, the sight of Lobster's phone on the nightstand killed the urge.

I pressed a key on the phone, a row of numbers popped out. I memorized them before pressing another key to wipe them out. Pure curiosity. I always wondered about the people Lobster knew. They were certainly capable.

XXII

Everything had gone smoothly yesterday until I found it hard to sleep at night. I was alone in my bed, whereas she was next door with Lobster. Although wide awake, I couldn't hear a thing from their room. All was quiet. The air conditioner hissed and pumped cool dry air into the room. My mouth went dry.

Everything had been on track during the day. When Lobster went out to get the item he ordered, I sat with her in the room. We did nothing but talk, because shortly afterwards Lao Xu called. We didn't talk about anything of consequence, because what happened between us went beyond words. But Lao Xu called, so in fact I didn't kiss her properly. It was nice when she let me kiss her, though. Her lips felt cool. When they were wet they felt as soft and sticky as a glutinous dumpling. I tucked them between my lips until her tongue parted my mouth. She was sitting on the sofa and I was kneeling between her legs. I wanted to reach down her back below the waistband of her skirt. Actually I had already located the zipper, but I didn't pull it down. Instead my fingers probed between the cushion and her bottom. I could feel her pull herself straight, but with half of my weight on her she hardly succeeded.

Then Lao Xu called. I went downstairs. When I went up again, Lobster had returned. What was inside the envelope he had brought back gave me some relief. Upon closer examination I felt like having a straight flush in a card game. I even proposed that we had the game played out the same night, but Lobster disagreed. He kept his pace. That was his strong suit. Old hands like him never improvise. Improvisation chases after nothing but one or two ambiguous motives. If you really want something done, you'd better follow a plan.

I didn't reveal much to Lao Xu about the upcoming business deal. There was no point doing so. The dinner party last night was no different from any other party. We ate, drank and spun stories. Only the participants were different. All was well as long as Lao Xu had fun. A person could easily brew hostility against others when he is surrounded by strangers in a strange place. To let him off his guard, you must provide him with some fun.

What was really worth telling about last night was just an intuition. I shouldn't discuss it because it was none of my business. Mind you, I was by no means incurious. I was always curious about what happened behind my back. I picked up some signals. At first, Xiao Mi received a phone call at dinner, which was quite commonplace. Who doesn't take calls at meals? She spoke falteringly before leaving the table to talk behind a bulky column at the entrance, but I didn't give it much thought. Ten minutes later, she came back. What happened next caught my attention. Her phone kept ringing, but instead of picking it up she just showed it to Lobster. Lobster made no comment other than saying, "Why don't you mute it?" She switched it to vibrant mode, but I could hear the vibration, because the purse containing her phone rested on the unoccupied chair next to me.

After dinner it became more interesting. Lao Xu was enjoying himself, so I could shift my attention elsewhere. The interesting fact was that Lobster and Xiao Mi left us in a private karaoke room of a night club for an entire hour. Others in the gang were busy singing, playing finger-guessing games, throwing dices, and drinking. I drank too, but I did little else.

They acted normal when they came back, but knowing them well I could smell that something had happened between them. Xiao Mi was preoccupied, while Lobster was slow in response. He used to be boisterous on such occasions. His good memory allowed him to tell one dirty joke after another, stirring the lust of his audience, male and female alike. However, right now it took him several seconds to realize that someone had just told a brand new dirty joke. "Sorry, say it again?"

So I could tell something had happened between the two of them. Assuming myself to be the cause of their tension, I was somewhat nervous. However, shortly afterwards she came to sit by me, so it was not about me. Although she didn't talk much, she was agreeable to my offer of drinks and cigarettes, her right leg pressed tightly against my left leg. She was not one of those women who pretended to be intimate with a man in order to piss off another man she had just fought with. She was not petty like that.

On the other hand, Lobster was petty enough to make out with a woman in order to piss off another woman he had just fought with. The room where we were abounded in women, but he made no move. So the tension was truly not about me.

Relaxed, I played tricks with cigarettes. The moment I lit one Xiao Mi would take it away, but before she put it between her lips I had another one in my hand. It was a simple trick. I just had to hide the second cigarette in my palm. Yet women were always delighted.

That was all about yesterday. Now, about today, this Friday. By evening the circus would be packed, all stage props would lie ready backstage, and the magician was about to enter on the stage. Before he made his appearance the clown would cry, "The show is on." The magician had better get into the mood even if he was jaded by now, because his mood would be contagious.

It was three in the afternoon, I was in bed with just a pair of briefs. The October sun felt as scorching as ever when it reached my bare torso. Lao Xu had been holed up in his room since last night without making a single outbound call. At 11 a.m., I ordered room service for him. After lunch, the other two guys vanished too. That was the cost you had to pay for hitching up with your friend's girl. That was the bullet you had to bite.

The sun shone on my face. I closed my eyes. Numerous golden stars danced before me.

XXIII

We were in a private room of another restaurant. The theme color was dark green. A golden strip skirted the green wallboard at around two meters above the floor. Both the tablecloth and chair covers were dark green velvet with golden stripes. The same went for the sofa. In addition, the metal legs of the glass coffee table, all table legs and chair legs were painted with a dubious golden color. However, the room was by no means bright. The light was dim, and the golden furnishings were darkened or blotched by age.

The round table was big enough to seat fifteen brawny men. The room was big enough to accommodate two more such tables. Even so, there were not many patrons. The two guys who, according to Lobster, could ship cases of cell phones here on demand were perched on the two innermost chairs facing the door. Their thick gold chains and huge gold watches not only matched well with the room, but also lent splendor to it. To their right were Lobster, Lao Xu and Lao Xu's temporary date, in proper order. To their left were two empty chairs and then Xiao Mi. I sat beside the door, with three vacant chairs on both sides, commanding an arc of about two hundred degrees out of the entire circumference of the table.

To be frank, I was not a gifted magician. Beneath the placatory surface of dinner there was an undercurrent of tension and restlessness. Among the few that sensed the undercurrent, Lobster was the most aplomb. As he browsed the menu he reminisced with the two guys who were as tacky as their jewelry while as fortified as a bank vault. The story sounded like an episode in a Kung Fu novel. Once upon a time, a broke Lobster was drinking alone in a small restaurant in Guangzhou. One of the two guys happened to be another lonely soul at the next table. They struck up a conversation. When they found out their shared passion for hotpots, they left their respective food for a hotpot place. At that time the Taiwanese guy didn't know how smart Lobster was; neither did Lobster have any idea of the weight the guy carried in Taiwan. Anyway, a night of drinking was enough to make them brothers. Moreover, since their encounter coincided with the wave of offshore expansion of Taiwanese hustlers, they were literally the frontiersmen.

Judged by their facial muscles, the two guys must be taken seriously. They had weathered faces with grooves that were indistinguishable from scars. However, their presence weakened as soon as they spoke, because their mandarin was broken, and their tones were soft and affectedly sweet.

They were discussing business details, things like delivery date and place, money order and bill of landing. Their "and" sounded like "hand", tables "hand" chairs, men "hand" women. Shit, what kind of mandarin was that! It was so hard to repress the urge to ask them, "Left hand or right hand?"

Business talk came to a conclusion when the waiter inquired about our beverage choices. Lobster warned Lao Xu against having beer and seafood at the same time. He said such a diet would cause gout and swell a man's toes into the size of his penis. He even addressed Lao Xu's temporary date, "Who can handle toes as big as one's penis?"

By contrast, Xiao Mi was not herself. I could tell. After all I knew her so well. If it was up to me, I'd rather keep her in the dark.

As for me, of course I was well aware of what was about to happen, but I suddenly felt helpless. This was no time for moral principles. I had known that for ten, twenty years. The sense of helplessness was commonplace when I sat for exams in school. The cheat sheets I had painstakingly prepared the night before were arranged neatly in the left pocket of my orange jacket, but I had no idea how to get them out without being noticed. The night before, the plan had seemed perfect: with several well categorized cheat sheets of fine print hidden under the test paper, I could sail through the exam. However, in the exam room I dared not reach my left hand into the pocket. I had placed the cheat sheets in the left pocket because during the exam my left hand, unlike the right hand, didn't hold any pen. I made numerous mental calculations at the expense of getting the sheets out real quick. Consequently, the sheets were of no help, and whatever there was in my memory was beyond recall.

When it was time to sum up the lessons learned, I knew very well that this was an issue of neither moral principles nor balls. Instead it was purely technical. A plan in your head and its execution were two different things.

The liquor bottle on the table went dry. A waiter came to open another one. I was not thirsty at all.

For a while things stood still. What should be said had been said, but what should be done had not been done at all. An awkward silence reined the room for a few minutes before Xiao Mi broke it, "*The Million Pound Note*. I have never seen so much money except in the movie."

To be honest, I'd rather keep her in the dark, but Lobster was right. Sometimes, especially when an abrupt turn of event is essential, women come in handy. They may hesitate, but they are ruthless when you need a nudge.

"You haven't seen that much money. She did," Lobster said. "Right? You did see it." He was addressing the woman beside Lao Xu.

"What?" The woman widened her eyes like a movie star in front of a camera, although her smile was by no means star quality. Her eyebrows arched a bit too much, and too many teeth were visible. However, I heard that Lao Xu and his peers in their forties liked such smiles. While smiling, she straightened her back and her right hand tucked at her sparkling silver belt.

"We're talking about money. Why did you tuck your pants?"

"I didn't." The woman joined the chorus of laughter. What a silly chick.

Lao Xu was laughing too. He must have enjoyed himself these past few days. A small black bag sat on the empty chair to the left of his girl. It had been with him since we met in Lao Cao's office. I suspected that he brought it to the bathroom. Maybe that woman had used it as a pillow, so that he would be assured even in his wildest moments. Right now the bag was still in his view, so apparently it was safe.

"I can't believe it. He must have shown you," Lobster yelled.

Lao Xu gulped down some liquor. His toothy grin made him sillier than before.

"This works better than any knockout drops. With one look she will do whatever you want her to do."

"What are you talking about? I swear I haven't seen it," said the woman.

Upon the insistence of all others Lao Xu reached over her thighs for the black bag.

He opened the bag, unzipped an inside pocket, and withdrew an envelope. I had guessed right. People like Lao Xu itemized. They kept things in envelopes. Up till now there should be just one crease line on that piece of paper, the one I created by folding it in two on the bank counter before handing it to Lao Cao.

That piece of paper was the one million yuan money order issued out of a special account whose serial number started with 127. Anyone who presented Lao Xu's ID card to a bank teller would be able to transfer the money to another account or simply cash it out. Lao Xu handed it to his chick, basking in the glory. Their eyes locked momentarily, agreeing tacitly on another round of uninhibited fun. I seized the opportunity to fish out a piece of paper from my linen jacket draped over my chair. I moved gingerly, because I didn't want anyone to notice, neither did I want to wrinkle it. I had folded it in two. Now it was on my lap beneath the napkin.

Later, the woman passed the money order to me. I reached a hand out without moving the upper part of my body since I didn't want to the napkin to slip. I admired the front side of the money order and then flipped it over. My memory had not failed me. The font was right, the ink might be slightly different, but it didn't matter. Something else seemed wrong. What was it? I couldn't locate it, maybe it was just hypochondria.

I raised the glass for a sip. The money order dropped onto my lap.

Lobster said, "See. It not only gets women high. He can't even hold it steady." Everybody burst out laughing. The money order was back in my hand. I hesitated. Should I surrender it now? How many seconds were sufficient to wipe it out of others' short-term memory? I had acted nimbly, but my arm might have moved, and someone might have seen it out of the corner of his eyes. It might sink into oblivion, or it might rouse him from sleep.

Xiao Mi came to my rescue. She took the money order from me. After taking a look her enthusiasm was immediately deflated. She tossed it back to Lao Xu. We soon started another topic.

XXIV

It all started with Lobster's desire for one million yuan. One million was not an astronomical amount, but we simply didn't have it. As a matter of fact, we had never possessed such an amount of money, even if millions had passed through us from time to time. The night when Lobster led a gang to the fishing village but came back empty-handed, Lobster told me, "It's easy. He just has to believe money is still in his hands."

We needed to create in the mind of Lao Cao (or in the current circumstances, Lao Xu) an illusion of possession. Two things were critical: firstly, I must have superb retention. I must memorize, within seconds, all details of that money order, including the type of paper, color, content, font, and in particular, the occasional spots and marks on the paper, which were more important than names and numbers. Who could tell what Lao Xu saw on the money order and transcribed into his double-entry bookkeeping mind? I didn't really worry about the number. Lao Xu was an accountant. In his profession, what was written down on paper was always truer than what was in one's memory. I, on the other hand, would rather trust my brain. According to Lü Yan, I was a good card player too.

A veteran card player had taught me a few tricks before. He was known as the master card player west of Xizang Road and south of Beijing Road. He regarded other parts of Shanghai with contempt, because, in his opinion, players there were more bandits than masters. He once tossed a pack of cards on the table for me to reshuffle. Then he cut the deck with a cigarette dangling from his lips as if he were God of Gamblers in the movie. I kept time. It took him only 53 seconds to shuffle the cards into the order he fancied. For him, four flushes were the easiest. He also claimed that he could, depending on the number of players, shuffle the cards in such a way that all trump cards and aces would be dealt to him. "It was purely a matter of memory," he said.

Secondly, we needed a master forger. Unlike con artists peddling false papers in the street, true masters only took orders from reputable clients. Lobster could fix it. He knew which phone numbers to call. Instead of saving those numbers in his phone, he relied on his memory (which is again proof of his trustworthiness).

No master could forge a money order identical to the one in Lao Xu's possession. However, Lao Xu would never see two money orders at the same time. What posed threat was his memory, not the authentic money order. There were always things beyond your control, like the inexplicable "retinal memory".

Fate was sealed in a snap. If nobody raised objections when the fake money order was returned to Lao Xu, then nobody would ever detect it.

The authentic money order, the one million yuan check that could be withdrawn, transferred and cashed out at any time, was now in my possession. I must guard it jealously. I must monitor closely the entire process of picking up delivery, making payment and transporting the goods to Lao Cao's warehouse. There was a world of difference between playing a trick on a friend and setting a trap for him. The weight on my shoulders felt heavy. I took the money order out of my jacket pocket and inserted it gingerly under the mattress. It nestled about twenty centimeters from the edge, beyond the reach of any maid who came in to make the bed.

I had returned to my room at around eleven in the evening. Ten minutes later, Lobster knocked at my door. He came in with a serious look typical of card players who got a good hand.

His eyes betrayed him. Alcohol and something else had made them bright and watery. From my angle they were even evasive.

"You were not bad at all," Lobster commented.

I sniggered. The comic sense was overwhelming. Didn't it all look like a play? I laughed until I collapsed onto the small sofa. By and by I calmed down.

Occasional hysteria like that is good to your mental and physiological health. If you are focused on something, you'll sooner or later develop an illusion. If you laugh like I did, the illusion will be ripped apart, and reality will rush in.

You will see my point if you regard your life as a card game. Playing cards does exercise one's mind. It takes a good brain to play well. Got it? I mean, with a good hand you may design many moves, but eventually there is only one right move. One move, one set of logic. All others are wrong. You may argue that there are exceptions, and that the best hand can be played out in many ways. Actually, come to think of it, you are wrong. If you have the best hand possible, then you should aim at winning all stakes or a grand slam. You should bait others into betting everything they own down to their boxers, and eventually take all. Therefore, at the end of the day, there is only one way to play. However, life is not a card game. In life you can make do with imperfection.

I didn't explain to Lobster why I laughed. We had always had a tacit understanding.

Sophisticated as he was, he didn't ask for the money order. How long and how much does it take to master such skills? You have a good hand, but you refrain from looking at it. Despite the turmoil inside you sit there solemnly, smoking, banging the table and telling petty jokes,

I fished the money order from under the mattress, held it in two fingers and flapped it in the air, as if tempting a dog with a bone. Something snagged at me. I examined the paper closely under the lamp. The writing was clear, bold and unequivocal.

I passed it to Lobster. "Will you look at it? Something is wrong with the one you made."

Lobster couldn't see anything odd. After turning it over and over again, he told me, "It's all right. I can't tell the difference. Even if something is wrong, Lao Xu can't spot it. He won't. He will never compare them side by side."

He was right. Nobody could do anything even if there was a slight inconsistency. What was the term? The blind spot?

"Another ID card has been made too. We must get the authentic one from Lao Xu."

"Can't we just use the fake one at the bank?"

"No, we must have the authentic one, even if bank tellers can't see the difference. Authentic money order and authentic ID card. No traces left."

Do you see how meticulous a good card player is? I had already sent a copy of Lao Xu's ID card to Lobster when I checked him into the hotel in Fuzhou. With that Lobster had a duplicate made. It was not a shoddy reproduction at all. You could almost consider it a work of art. Young girls working at the bank would never challenge it. Afterwards, when Lao Cao received the goods and when the other party received money, who would care about a fake ID? Nevertheless, a good card player like Lobster would never allow any unnecessary loophole.

XXV

I had slept soundly last night, the kind of slumber you slipped into after getting over some big stress. Before falling asleep, when my body grew increasingly heavy and my auditory sense was temporarily sharpened, I heard a man and a woman talk. Their voices flowed in through the window, so I couldn't say for sure whether they came from Lobster's room.

When I woke up after five in the morning, I stumbled into the shower to have a very hot soak. The night wind had infiltrated the sheets and made my skin tingle. Then I lied down again to read a few pages of the novel I picked up from the floor. Then I was asleep once more. I didn't get up until around nine.

I finished breakfast around ten thirty. Nobody sought me out. I tried to make myself busy in the hotel, having a massage on this floor and a glass of tonic water on another. Nobody came to see me. They had vanished as if they needed to lie low after something major. I had thought others would become as excited as I was when they got the money order, yelling, dancing around it, drinking, and laughing heartily. But the truth was they seemed to have suddenly lost interest.

I sat around until three.

I could tell the time relatively precisely because, feeling my cheeks flushed after two glass of gin tonic, I checked my watch and decided to leave the hotel lobby bar for somewhere else to kill the couple of hours before supper. Just at that time I saw Xiao Mi emerge out of an elevator with the determined look of a patient walking into a dentist's clinic. She proceeded without hesitation towards the revolving door, swirled out, and crossed the hotel driveway to hail taxi from the curb.

I beckoned the waiter for the bill. A game of shadowing seemed to be fun.

My taxi driver almost lost Xiao Mi at the first turn, because there were two identical yellow Santanas about one hundred meters ahead of us when we swerved around. He might be pretending, because he had regarded me with suspicion when I told him to follow the yellow taxi in front of us. I had yelled happily to him, "Follow it closely. Don't let them shake us off."

Car tracing was not as simple as you saw in movies. You always felt that the other party had seen you. You didn't know what to do whenever he accelerated or decelerated. Should you follow suit or simply overtake him? You would think every maneuver by the other's driver was targeted at you, but in fact it was unintended.

Xiao Mi's taxi pulled over in front of a bank. She got off to stand at the steps, her thin skirt billowing in the warm breeze. I told my cabbie to wait on the opposite side of the street. To placate him I also passed along a one hundred yuan bill. From where I sat in the taxi, I could see her profile facing the wind. I knew the body underneath that skirt with black patterns on a white background. The breezes that caressed her body were like the strokes of a telepathist sketcher who knew what I was thinking.

After ten minutes she started to look about. At about four in the afternoon she came down the steps to hail another taxi.

I lost her. My cabbie had had enough. After making a turn at a crossroads, he slammed the brakes on so abruptly that we almost ran into the sidewalk. The curses he flung at me in the local dialect were all Greek to me. He got off the car, circled around the front to yank open the door on my side. I got off in anticipation of a fist fight, yet apparently he just wanted me out. No sooner had I planted my feet on the ground than he went back to his seat relieved.

The odor in the air reminded me that summer had not left this southern city even if it was already October. It was a smell oozing out of walls, a mixture of rotten fruit and human sweat. I didn't return to the hotel until it got dark. I sat on the edge of the bed, inserting my right hand between the nightstand and the bed. With two fingers I felt for the money order under the mattress. It was there. I had put it there in front of Lobster the other night. It felt no different from a label stuck to the back of the mattress or a sheet of instructions on how to use condoms left there by a previous guest.

A few minutes later, I went to ring the doorbell next door. I rang thrice. Nobody answered it.

It occurred to me that I hadn't thought about Lao Xu the whole day. This was a sign of unsophistication, an indication that I was feeling guilty subconsciously. I dialed Lao Xu's room number. He didn't pick up.

I was lying on top of a piece of paper worth a million yuan. It was right there under my back. Despite the mattress I could feel it. Although Lobster had been out of sight the whole day, I believed his heart was always with this piece of paper. The phone rang. It was Lobster.

"Where have you been?"

"I called you before supper."

I took out my cell phone from an inside pocket of my jacket. It was out of power.

"I haven't seen you the whole day. I'm with the money. If you don't show up, I will bring it to the airport."

"Take it easy. Get something to drink downstairs."

Although I was not as high as he imagined, my body temperature did go up slightly with one million yuan under my buttocks.

"I won't return to the hotel tonight. I'm heading out for Fuqing."

He didn't mention Xiao Mi. It was a Saturday. In the humid

darkness outside, neon lights outlined streets, taxies shuttled back and forth carrying passengers on their way to a night of fun. I kicked off my shoes, removed the dead phone battery for recharging after replacing it with a standby. I switched on the TV to channel surf. Lo Ta-yu was singing *A Moment Like This*. I dropped the remote control.

I called room service for some wonton noodles. I didn't call Xiao Mi because she might be with Lobster. Besides, I didn't know whether it was OK to call her. Two slices of star fruit floated in the noodle soup. Was it Taiwanese cuisine? Or Thai? There was a sour and bitter taste in my mouth. I needed a bottle of Chivas Regal.

I drank sitting on the bed. A cigarette was burning in the ashtray. My eyes were teary from the smoke. Nevertheless, it was a warm tender night. The whiskey was good. I stared at the set of sofas by the window. The fabric was covered with dark green and golden stripes. The interior designer must be a huge fan of these two colors. I liked the sofa cover. It reminded me of Ernst Lubitsch and one of his movies.

I liked the German director for the lonely souls as well as the dark green sofa in his movies. Right now, drinking whiskey alone in my room with a million-yuan note under the mattress, I seemed to be one of his characters. If he were the director, in the next scene a woman would walk in to sit on the sofa. However, although I kept drinking until eleven, no woman walked in or called.

XXVI

Someone roused me from sleep. When I opened my eyes, the moonlight was swinging like wine in a glass. Darkness poured in from the window, painting the walls of the room purple. A dark figure was squatting by me. Despite my drowsiness I knew it was Xiao Mi. She pressed her face against my nose. I smelled the fumes of whiskey from my own mouth. Lobster had a key to this room. I had left it with him before flying to Shanghai.

A voluptuous woman dressed in black appearing by our bedside, wasn't it every man's fantasy coming true? We—the average men in this world, including Pu Songling[1] and Raymond Chandler—were bolder when half awake.

For a couple of minutes I could hardly catch my breath. At night, abruptly deprived of sleep, one felt disoriented but a hundred times more acute in touching. Without myself realizing it I was groping her all over. My hands and my half-awake brain seemed to be a thousand kilometers apart, yet they were also connected by something like a superconductor. Upon touching her skin an electric current rushed toward my brain at light speed, dashing against the innermost part under the cranium. From the epicenter came tremor upon tremor.

"Given an arc, how can we locate the center of the circle?" I

---

1   Pu Songlin (1640–1715) was a Qing Dynasty ghost story writer. A frequent theme in his stories was a female ghost or fox coming into the study of a scholar and falling in love with him.—*Trans.*

heard myself mumble as if I was talking in sleep.

"What?"

"Nothing." I laughed at my own idiocy. Now I was much awake.

I groped her desperately. My hand slid between her legs and felt a wet warm spot against the cotton pants. Like a jazz musician hastening out to perform, I found the right rhythm after banging around for a while. Now, my right hand was gliding over the higher notes and my left hand was clapping the lower notes. I tried in vain to pull down her pants. She wriggled against me. I pushed her up in order to unbutton her, but she misunderstood. She wriggled down, hooking her fingers to remove my briefs. Despite our entangled bodies I could see my erection in the darkness.

My head had not fully cleared up, but I was well aware that she didn't come with me. It was not entirely my fault. She had been hot, using her hands and mouth, and then sitting on me like a fretted British shorthair.

She straddled me to reach for a cigarette. I rolled over to bury my face in the pillow. My plea for a cigarette sounded like a mumble. She kicked me on the ass. I turned around to see her left leg on the floor, her right leg on me, and a black patch in between. I reached out for the patch. She twisted her body away while putting a cigarette in my mouth.

Now she was sitting naked on the sofa. Between flickers I saw her reclining figure in the moonlight, her right leg on the armrest, her belly flesh forming two soft bulges. She was looking at me as if deep in thought.

As I smoked I made faces at her belly button. She couldn't see me, though. There were creases above and below it. They extended sideways to her flanks. She was seated in the middle of the dark green sofa, her bottom pressed closely against the coarse fabric. The skin I had just caressed was now on intimate terms with the ice-cold fabric. She looked like a slut.

I leapt at her. I knelt between her legs, grabbing her knees and biting her belly. She grabbed my hair with one hand and lifting my jaw with another. My face was upturned. She licked my lips. My hands went beneath her bottom. Now my palms separated the coarse fabric from her smooth bottom. I kissed her all over. When I proceeded to her belly she said, "What you have is fake."

I bit her vehemently at the lower part of the belly. The friction between teeth and hair was audible. It had dawned on me almost immediately, but instead of sobering up I felt dizzier than before. Holding her higher up, I kissed her private parts repeatedly. I had never thought of doing so on account of Lobster and my mysophobia.

I kept kissing it while scratching her ass and legs with my fingernails until she came. I could almost hear her orgasm because my ears were squeezed right between her legs.

She lay in the pool of lamplight, her breath short and the cigarette butt flickering. I lay on my back beside her, waiting for her to break the silence.

"Lobster ordered two fake checks."

Her legs softened up under my caress. I lay there like an exhausted man, touching her from time to time as she explained the intricacy of the matter, trying to detect her evasion. Strangely, I didn't care much about the trick Lobster had played on me. It was bound to happen. A different kind of fear loomed over me. However, owing to the clandestine nature of our relationship, I couldn't ask her for clarification bluntly. Maybe it was wrong to ask even between lovers.

She had not dried up yet down there. A question came out of my mouth. "Was it you? At dinner?"

Her legs pinched my fingers slightly. She turned to look at me without speaking.

I was gullible, I wanted to be gullible. But she just looked at me with loving eyes. I returned the look. My fingers spoke for me. She was wet again.

I wanted it to harden and harden some more, but it didn't.

Then I asked, "Were you in it from the very beginning?"

She kissed me, her hand clasped around my penis. Then she slid down to rest her head on my belly. She regarded it, played with it, and then nodded her head.

I straddled her, parting her legs brutally. I patted her private parts.

"Was it also part of the plan?"

She shoved my arms glaring at me, "Think what you want."

"OK." I crossed my legs and lit another cigarette. "What made you tell me now? What has Lobster done to you? Do you need my help?"

She propped herself up on an arm and curled her right leg, as if she was resting gracefully on a rock on the seaside.

I patted her cheek, removing a strand of hair from the corner of her mouth. I couldn't help putting on a sinister smile. "Well, well, the losses are not mine. What do you want from me?"

"What do I want from you? Stop pretending. You should be more like him. A tough guy takes whatever measure necessary. If kneeling helps, you kneel. When crying and screaming works, you cry and scream. That's what a tough guy does." She muttered angrily at me under her breath. With laughter I took her into my arms, kissing her and touching her.

In fact I was not really turned on.

XXVII

"I need lots of money," Xiao Mi spoke under me. Her voice seemed to come out of a damp cave.

"How much? One million?"

"My bar will be completed very soon. I've lots of bills to pay."

It took her half an hour to tell the story. We had had sex again, but I didn't withdraw from her, as if such a posture made her story more credible. So far, sex was the only thing I still believed in. Her gasps, moans, and orgasms couldn't be faked, right? Of course I knew they could be faked too. Women can always spin and reel at the same time, can't they? Men think with either their head or their penis. The problem is, a woman is like a receptacle that contains more than you. You push and push trying to invade as much territory as possible, but you never know how much is left unoccupied.

"Lobster saw to the down payment. Back then he was rich. He offered to help me start a bar. After the lease was signed he ran into trouble. All my money was in the project. The bar is going to open very soon, but there is one last bill."

"So there are no cell phones from Taiwan at all?"

"He is in a deep hole. Other than debts he was also caught with some false bank paper."

"He has never done that before."

"He's at his wit's end. They have the false paper on him."

"So he cheated on you too? He talked you into trapping me

and then tried to dump you? Then you have to come back to me. Is that right?"

"I saw him through. He promised them on the phone that everything would be settled next week. After getting the money order he tried to dodge me. He no longer talked about what to do next. I also knew he slipped away to book just one plane ticket."

I liked her candidness. Under such circumstances such effrontery is appreciated. I had lied to you, but when I found out it did me no good, I warned you against it. I kissed her with my parched lips. Her nipples were as soft as premium rubber. She pinched my ass. It was not a sign of impatience, but of carelessness.

It was time to scare her, I decided. A strange relief came over me. I wanted to tease someone, whoever he or she was. I told her, "Lobster knows the money order in his hand is authentic, while Lao Xu and I have fake ones. He also knows you know. Do you really believe he has gone to Fuqing? He must have people watching us. Maybe he is watching us now, right in this hotel. And look at us, naked in bed. Maybe he is secretly taping us. Good porn material. "

"Or maybe it's X-rated." I offered an afterthought as I jammed her with my belly.

The soft flesh beneath me suddenly went rigid. She curled her legs tightly around my hip. There was a vacant look on her face, and then there was a slight trace of dejection. She looked at the ceiling. "Why did he do this to me?"

"Why did you do this to him?" I snickered.

"He is seeing other women. All these three years since we've been together, he was clean only the first three months. Every time he fucked me, I wondered where his penis had just been."

I could live with such an explanation. Women always use it as a last resort. I don't think it's cliché. After all, women care about it.

A night wind had risen. Despite the closed windows we

could feel the air whizzing by. How was Lobster monitoring us? We looked at each other until our shoulders felt the chill. She wrapped herself around me, her wound-like slit pressed tightly against my groin, as if it were an air valve that, once, released, would deflate her like an inflatable doll until she became a sheet of flattened plastic.

"Fuck me again." Her eyes were bright and willful.

I lay in bed. With Xiao Mi beside me, I felt good even if there were numerous eyes spying on us, because we could start dreaming a new dream. A moment ago, right before her orgasm, she wailed, "How much money do you have?"

Such a question might dispirit other men, but I penetrated her with even greater force. In pace with the rhythmic thrust I asked her, "How much do you need? How much do you need? How much do you need?"

I didn't blame her for mentioning money then and there. Money is always an important factor in your dreams. Money is like a big stone tossed into the small pond that was dream. Without it the pond wouldn't stir at all.

I lit a cigarette. White smoke rings helped me think better. Vehicles passed by from time to time. They were not heavy-duty ones, because the rustle of tires was gentler than that of leaves.

"He doesn't know your suspicion, does he?"

Xiao Mi seemed to be dazed. She was looking at the ceiling without seeing it.

"I say, he doesn't know you know he's booked only one ticket. He doesn't know you are suspicious, right?"

"What do you mean?"

"I'm thinking."

I had a preliminary plan. There was a big loophole somewhere in Lobster's otherwise perfect plan. He took advantage of me because he had sensed my yearning for his girl. He had probably sensed it before I did.

He allowed Xiao Mi to seduce me—I didn't know if he had given Xiao Mi explicit instructions, but I wouldn't ask her anyway. Then he had us kidnapped. With a nudge from Xiao Mi on that typhoon night I started to play his game willingly. I had not always been that obliging. Certainly Xiao Mi had seen the kidnapping coming, so she was not scared. I had admired her for that. Remember? She had only complained about no showers or clean change of underwear.

He hadn't expected Xiao Mi to sleep with me. It was unlike him to include such a possibility in his plan. I was not saying he didn't have the heart to do so. Big time gamblers like him bet on anything. However, it was exactly because he was a big-time gambler that he couldn't imagine Xiao Mi falling for me. He was confident in his own charm. Of course, he could be confident in another way, i.e., Xiao Mi would still on his side even if she slept with me. Out of the two versions, I was inclined to the former.

So there was a loophole. He would be screwed if Xiao Mi took my side. If she meant what she had said on that magic night, then things might come to a different end. There was a big bang. Xiao Mi shivered slightly. The ash from my cigarette dropped onto the hollow of her shoulder.

My train of thought was disrupted. However, when I brushed the ash off her shoulder, contrarian thinking took place in my head.

XXVIII

The scenes that night flashed across my mind. Xiao Mi said, *"The Million Pound Note ..."* Lao Xu took the money order out of the black bag. Now the money order was in my hand. It fell onto my lap. I hesitated. I wanted to slip it into my pocket and take the fake one from under my napkin. But everybody was looking and I had only three fingers hidden beneath the napkin. The fake money order folded in two was inserted into the real one similarly folded into two. I handed them to Xiao Mi. She tossed one of them to Lao Xu. As for the other one, she stuffed it into my pocket when we bumped into each other outside the bathroom.

The money order must first of all come back to me, because I must be implicated. Later, Lao Xu would recall how it fell onto my lap. Swapping the two checks on my own had been our Plan A, and Xiao Mi's intervention, Plan B. However, even if I hadn't managed the swap, Lao Cao would still point his finger at me. Then there would be some leeway. Even if Lao Cao found out about our plan, he wouldn't call the police. Instead he would confront me. Then we could negotiate with him because we had one million yuan.

If the real money order had been in my pocket, Xiao Mi had numerous opportunities to replace it with a fake. Lobster hadn't expected me to put the money order under the mattress, which was beyond his imagination. But anyway, if I had had the real money order, Lobster would get hold of it eventually, via

Xiao Mi, of course, since I couldn't wait—Lobster was aware of that—I couldn't wait to surrender my briefs to Xiao Mi, let alone a piece of paper.

There were three money orders, one real and two others fake. I knew it instantaneously when Xiao Mi said, "What you have is fake." The trick was neither novel nor sophisticated. Any street bum would know it. Have you fallen victim to such a hoax at street corners? Three cards were laid out in front of you. You stared at one without blinking your eyes, thinking you would never lose track of it. The hoaxer shuffled the three cards this way and that way before laying them out again. You were confident since the card you wanted had never been out of your sight. You pointed at it, this one, right there. You put down a stake. He flipped the card. You were wrong. You always lost.

So, back to square one. She didn't come tonight to commit adultery. She had come to pass the buck. Like a slippery white fish, she swam to me across the pool of darkness with an offer. She didn't want me to blow the whistle. Indeed there was still time to do that. I could get out. I could call Lao Cao, report the loss of the money order to the bank, or call the police.

She had greater confidence in herself than in me. She was indeed sure of herself.

However, I was not that sure. I jumped out of the bed to take a shower. When I came back she was still staring at the ceiling. I lit a cigarette for myself and another for her. It was time to talk business. I tossed the clothes piled on the floor to her. She had to at least put on her panties.

"Tell me about the bar."

Pushing aside the clothes, she went to sit on the sofa. The yellowish lamplight reflected off the floor shone on her left leg, lower abdomen and the back of the sofa. Her tuft of hair was too black and too shiny to ignore.

"The bar is mine on paper. All paperwork has been done with my ID." She began. I noticed her smooth abdomen. The two soft bulges were gone.

After she had finished, I went back to thinking. I had sorted it out when my hair was almost dry. There was still room for bargaining with Lao Cao if I got the one million yuan back. I could save this woman, or at least her bar.

But I didn't know if I could get the money back. The watch on the nightstand read Sunday. I had a day's time, but I must make up my mind now. It was a call to Lao Cao now or never.

"We can swap the money orders one more time." She came over to sit on my lap. She looked at me. I looked at her too. There was a sudden urge to slap her on the face. But she was sitting too close. In the end I slapped her on the butt.

I took the piece of paper from under the mattress to study it. I asked her, "How? Another sleight of hand? Breaking in or mugging him? Most likely he knows you're sleeping with me. Even if we make it, we may not walk out of this hotel. If Lobster could fake a kidnapping, he can do it for real."

An idea fleeted across my mind. It was like a scrap of burning paper fluttering in the air. The moment I reached out, it drifted away.

My heart raced. I pushed Xiao Mi aside and stood up. I poured some water and drank half a glass. I paced the floor in front of the bed barefoot, my footstep as light as that of a tomcat. I was restless like a tomcat as well, but not a tomcat in heat. The thing hung loosely from my groin like a used condom. Xiao Mi was regarding it with interest.

I needed fresh air. I went over to draw back the gauze curtain and throw open the window. A fog was rising. Streetlamps blinkered like they were on top of ship masts. A coarse voice was yelling. A woman was crying. I poked my head out. The deserted streets looked like a movie set. The wind blew through my half dry hair. I shivered happily. It was time to close the window.

Back in the bed, I studied the fake money order again. On all accounts it was perfect. The paper was stiff and smooth. The writing was distinct. The specimen seal impression for checking when making payment was bright-colored. Everything shouted "real".

The fleeting idea came back. I stared at the specimen seal impression. Come on, think hard, grasp it, don't let the idea go away again.

"What are you looking at?"

I brushed Xiao Mi's hand off without replying.

Something was wrong … I felt it upon first sight when Lobster produced the envelope … It was not the font, but the strokes. No, it was not the strokes either.

Then it dawned on me. My brain worked rapidly. A succession of details and assumptions fell into place. A plan emerged.

Half an hour later, I patted Xiao Mi on the cheek. Before speaking I lit up a cigarette and blew out a smoke ring, "There is a typo."

XXIX

When I woke up she was kneading my thing to make it rise. I pushed her away, leapt out of bed and headed for the bathroom. I ordered as I brushed my teeth, "Get up. We've a lot to do today."

I dressed at the entrance to the bathroom. Xiao Mi sat on the toilet not having a stitch on. I told her, "Let's go down for breakfast. When we are in the restaurant, kiss me and touch me down there. It's the best if Lobster's men see us. Afterwards you track down that woman, and I see to my business."

"How will you find that guy?"

"I have his phone number."

Her eyes widened in disbelief, which was quite comical accompanied by the flush of the toilet. I laughed. "I've got a good memory."

As we walked out of our room I looked around. The corridor was empty except for a cart overflowing with towels and toothbrushes at a corner. The maid was nowhere to be seen.

We left the elevator. It was a very quiet morning. Few guests were in the lobby. Several of them sat on sofas, one of whom was smoking and looking around. Two others stood with their luggage at the reception. People glanced at us, but none of them seemed to be particularly intense.

Except the guy who was smoking. I stared at him. He looked away. I heard people greeting each other under the chandelier, hello, thank you, blah, blah, blah. A newspaper ruffled as crisply as ice cracking. My throat went dry, as if I had accidentally walked into a touch-and-go confrontation between two gangsters. Numerous eyes seemed to be watching us from under the counters and behind the sofas.

I put my right hand on the small of Xiao Mi's back. The hollow there fit my palm well. Such intimacy was appropriate for the occasion. I mean, it was adequate to convince others that we were an illicit couple just out of bed.

The restaurant was more crowded. We shared a glass of juice, touching and kissing each other from time to time. Xiao Mi was carried away by acting. She even fed me the white meat of a razor clam with her fingers.

I didn't know who was watching us at the restaurant, but there must be someone. That was Lobster's style. He was always cautions. Anyway, the prospect of one million yuan outweighed anything else. He could well set aside one percent of it for a surveillance team.

I hoped that someone had seen us having an intimate breakfast. If after seeing us he called Lobster immediately, then Lobster must have been thinking since last night, especially since I took my seat at the restaurant about half an hour ago. That was step one.

Step one of my plan was to start Lobster thinking. Guys like him had a complicated mechanism in their head. Given some input, their brain would start processing. You never knew what the output would be. I must trigger the thinking process.

Xiao Mi and I parted company at the lobby. She had her own agenda, but first of all she had to go back to the room. I wandered out like a typical idler you saw who frequented high-end hotels around China. I told the taxi driver to take me to an art and craft store. Xiao Mi called when I was still in the taxi. No car left the hotel within two minutes of my departure.

Instead of going into the art and craft store, I lingered in front to make a call.

To my surprise, a woman answered. She spoke a loud

incomprehensible dialect. I wondered if she was cursing. I guessed wrong, because she soon switched to mandarin.

She got it as soon as mentioned Lobster's name. We both fell silent. There was a rustling noise in the phone, as if something was going to spout out. It might be emitted from a scrambler. I waited for her to speak. The arts and craft store was open, but tourists, who were the main patrons of such businesses, had not arrived yet. Salespeople, including women, stood leaning against shelves with hands in trouser pockets, the way street bums stood. I remained on the steps outside. The sun slanted through the awning onto my face. There were few pedestrians or cars in the street.

After about a minute or less, another person spoke on the other end of the phone. He spoke deliberately, ending each sentence with a note of uncertainty, as if he was not sure whether to make a statement or ask a question. I had to be patient.

I saw no point in a lengthy self-introduction. The more you talk about yourself, the more others want to know. I certainly didn't want him to call Lobster to know more about me. I simply said, "Lobster told me to find you." Before he could chew on it I said, "Give me your address. We'd better talk face to face." My voice was loud and clear. My tone was warm and cheerful.

When our conversation was over, I walked down the street, made a turn, picked up pace, jumped into a taxi, and gave the cabbie an address. Then I called Xiao Mi. According to her, Lao Xu was still in the room with his chick, and Lobster had called to announce his return after lunch.

The taxi drove along a wide road named Zhongshan Road, a common road name in Chinese cities, before turning into a narrow lane. It made its way through a wet market and then another turn. I got off.

I checked the street numbers of shops along the lane. The place should be here. Bikes crowded the lane. I needled through. Soon there were tire imprints on my Japanese cotton pants. The roller shutter door of a hair salon was pulled up halfway with a clatter. A girl emerged from under it. I saw her ass, then a short jean skirt, a pair of panties with floral patterns, and finally the water basin in her hands. I walked past as she emptied the basin into a gutter.

I located the book rental place. All but two pitted door panels in the middle had been folded back. The inside overflew with tattered Kung Fu novels. A passage in the back must lead to a room containing an old case of more expensive books for rent featuring a big long object.

A woman threw herself at me.

"What do you want?"

"Lobster told me to come," I said.

Shortly a man emerged into the dark passage. Wrinkled pajamas hung on his skinny body as if it were draped over the back of a cheap wooden chair. He beckoned me in. I crossed a small courtyard into a dark living room with smeared windows. Near the door there was a small table and several nylon and steel chairs. On the table was a tray of tea pot and cups. The electric kettle was whistling. He made me sit down.

Despite the suspicious stains inside the cup, I gulped down the scalding tea. Then I took out the sheet of paper from my wallet to show him the typo.

There should be an "o" instead of an "a" in the cashier's name on the specimen seal impression. It was hard to say whose fault it was now. Probably I was wrong when I drew the seal impression from memory, or it might be the guy in front of me.

XXX

In principle, forgers should not receive clients at home or any other permanent residence. God knows what clients will do with false papers! There are two kinds of forgers. The low-end ones stick flyers onto utility poles and walls in the small hours to avoid being seen. Clients call the number listed on the flyer. Shoddy goods and money change hands at street corners. The high-end ones are artists catering to carefully screened clientele with deep pockets. Both sides respect rules, keeping their mouths shut afterwards.

In this kind of long-term cooperation, both sides are in the same boat. Keeping secrets for one's partner equals keeping secrets for oneself. A person may be forced to tell, but he needn't reveal where he keeps the books, right?

My straightforward approach worked. The money order, which he knew better than anyone else, was the perfect letter of introduction.

Things went more smoothly than expected but for the price. Lobster didn't say how much he had paid. Never mind. I had it all planned out. Instead of making an offer I mentioned a detail. "How long does it take you to deliver on a rush order?"

"There is a rush fee."

"How much?"

"It's five thousand yuan between friends."

I agreed reluctantly to give him a sense of achievement.

He made me wait outside his studio. The pride of a

professional, I assumed. Artists are perfectionists. They can't stand intruders.

I didn't touch the pot of tea he had made for me before disappearing into his studio. The tea smelled good, but the tea cups were repelling. I had to survive on the last three cigarettes.

In the next two hours or so, my ass warmed the nylon cloth on all three uncomfortable chairs. I also figured out each and every character written in cursive hand in the traditional Chinese painting on the wall. I could even tell the number of grapes in it.

Finally, he walked out of the inner room bearing the object of my desire. I had stuffed five thousand yuan into an envelope to show my respect for an artist.

I handed him the envelope. With dignity he laid it beside the tea tray on the table. I admire his work. He stopped me from touching the writing. "Wait till it's dry."

On my way out I saw the same girl idle around inside the hair salon. Her gaudy underwear was again in sight, up front this time, because she sat facing the street with legs on another chair.

As soon as I walked into my hotel room, Lao Xu called. He was bored with little to do. His chick was playing local guide to Xiao Mi who asked her over lunch where to buy certain feminine products.

After a shower I opened a new packet of cigarettes. Xiao Mi called when I was smoking the first one. She said she would be back soon. Her voice sounded normal. Now the ball had been passed back to Lobster. I hoped he was not too mad. A man tends to lose his head when he learns about the affair between his woman and another man. However, Lobster was no ordinary man. I hoped that he remained cool, decisive, and more importantly, retentive.

I didn't call him. I was not sure about this. What if something I said aroused his suspicion? He would try to decipher my intention even if I simply wanted to know his time of return. No, I shouldn't influence his thinking. He had to figure it all out by himself. My job was to send a discreet signal in his direction one thousand meters away. The less said, the better.

I went over the plan again and again until my head hurt. The doorbell rang. Although not very loud, it made me flinch.

Xiao Mi entered. She took out a packet from her purse, threw the latter on the bed, and headed for the bathroom without forgetting to shut the door.

I finished smoking on the sofa. She walked over slowly. Then she squatted down, holding my face to look at her. Suddenly her kisses rained down. When I caught my breath she said, "I think I'm pregnant."

My head swam.

"The condom."

But that time—I caught myself before blurting it out. No, I was mistaken. Not the first time when we had sex without a condom, but the other time when I actually used one—the wrong-sized Okamoto. What an irony.

"That must be it." She stopped the pretended wail to echo my laughter. How frantic we had been when the condom went missing.

"It's true."

I don't know how other men react to similar news. It was just bad timing to me. Was it absolutely necessary? After all I had already agreed to help her. Fine, show me your pregnancy test result. I didn't care whether it was really positive.

I played according to her script. Even if I found it incredible, the show must go on. My logic was simple: she chose to tell me now because she wanted me to go all out for her; whereas I had already decided to help her. Therefore her pregnancy didn't make any difference. On second thought, it explained things. At least it was a plausible motive to people like Lao Cao.

She was smart whether she was truly pregnant or not. If it was true, her uterus was smart too.

"Shall I put my ear to your belly?"

"You cold-blooded bastard."

She stood up to drink from my water glass, looking sideways at me over its rim. I went around to embrace her. My hands rested on her hips.

"She wants to go to Shanghai."

Women sometimes switch subjects faster than you do. I hadn't had enough time to put on the look first of a man of grievance and then a man of responsibility. I looked at her, my chin on my hand, my elbow on the armrest of the sofa. She stood in front of me. Without the jutted out knees we could be even closer. My fingers worked at the lower hem of her blouse with black and white floral patterns. Part of her smooth abdomen came into view.

"She wants to go to Shanghai with Lao Xu, but Lao Xu doesn't agree."

"A good cause for a fight."

"Yeah. If my bar is up and running, she can work there."

Her bar would surely be up and running. The assertive tone in her voice was telling. She was wise in the ways of the world. Why hadn't I realized it before?

"Now, now, I have to look at you with new eyes."

XXXI

Lobster called after Xiao Mi had gone to book plane tickets. He was waiting for me in the bar downstairs. I rode the elevator alone. The mirror showed a pale face. The carriage dropped to the ground rapidly. I was a bit scared.

Lobster had ordered a drink for me. Chivas Regal was out of stock. The bartender served Dimple instead. I didn't like the bitter taste in my mouth. We sat beside the maroon glass wall. The afternoon sun leaked in. I didn't like maroon glass, either. It gave the room a cheap stale look. From the bar counter came the sound of an ice spade into an ice bucket and ice cubes into glass. Music floated from the ceiling. It was that well-known Scottish folk song. The string instruments were shrill and bitter, like a point blank irony.

"How was Fuqing? Have you seen the goods?" I heard the hollowness in my voice. Hidden beneath this worldly exterior and this painstakingly maintained image beat a coward's heart. I always wanted to run away from situations like this. Must we sit here drinking? You and I? After I knew you set me up to swindle one million out of Lao Cao? After you knew I slept with your woman?

What was on your mind? You smoke gloomily. You threw your head back to gulp half a glass of whiskey. With a roll of your tongue the liquor was down your throat. But what exactly was on your mind?

He looked at me blowing smoke rings. He cracked a smile.

"You need to get a good rest."

Strangely, I yawned, as if on cue.

"You didn't sleep well."

Silence. A sense of futility washed over me. Must I act all the way through? Could I bow out now? Could I toss the cigarette butt, drink up, get on my feet, dust ash off my clothes, and then tell him, "I know all your tricks. It's over. Let's be friends?"

He burst out laughing. There was a blur in his voice as if he had choked on the liquor. Then he said, "How was Xiao Mi? Ha ha ha—" He kept laughing chokingly, so much so that my throat felt dry and itchy too.

"I offered her to you before. You were such a hypocrite. I told you she was good, didn't I?"

What was going on? Did he try to claim the moral high ground?

"I didn't—"

I lowered my head to raise the glass. The golden liquid swirled inside. I started to speak but then stopped on second thought—it was just an act. You know that, right? In such circumstances denial is a way of acting as well as a sign of weakness. Am I right, Master Lobster? Have I overacted?

As such, you would believe I'm still in the dark about the money order. You know, Xiao Mi knows, but I don't. As such, my idiotic way of hiding the money order in a place both Xiao Mi and you know seems logical. Speaking of it, I was really an idiot to conceal the money order in such a place.

However, so far you have not got the whole picture. You've sensed something wrong, but you don't know what, until I send a signal to trigger your memory and your imagination. By then your meticulous mind would help me put an idea into your head and before your eyes.

"The best way to penetrate her is from behind. You'd better keep her on all fours." He kept laughing. His breaths squeezed out of his mouth together with smoke.

Then he stopped laughing and assumed a serious look. "Cut

the pretending. Women are nothing to me now. A couple of years ago, I cared. If you slept with my woman back then, I would have your dick fed to a dog."

I smoked and drank nonstop. The smoke twirled inside my mouth before getting out of my nose. The liquor barely wet my tongue. My eyes fell on a white rock in the yard. Its clean smooth surface was in contrast with the mossy bottom. A long-tailed bird perched on it.

"I've seen her through these past two years. She's got brains. Not a bad woman, but she has a mind of her own."

I refocused on him. "She does have a mind of her own."

"An unusual mind actually. You either make her a partner or tell her to get lost. Don't ever treat her like a wife, otherwise you have to guard against her constantly."

Unable to either agree with him or raise objections, I tapped the glass on the tablecloth to create some distraction.

"You can't reason with her or any other women. Neither can you be unreasonable. She has a mind of her own. You can't get tough with her. That's the delicate part." He leaned against his chair, his voice lower and lower, and his head drooped lower and lower too, as if he was thinking aloud, or his head were in consultation with his cock.

How brotherly we were, and how sentimental! I tried hard to immerse myself into the friendly atmosphere without going overboard. I had underestimated Lobster. His brain worked faster than I had imagined. Without realizing it he had approached the truth, the truth I wanted him to believe in.

You want to distract me and influence me. After Xiao Mi slept with me, you sensed she had her own agenda. You have been confident in your cock. You had thought it made Xiao Mi happy. If she sought another cock, she must have a purpose. Right? Somehow you expected to fall back on me one day.

So you really believe I'm still in the dark like an idiot. I thought a bit peevishly.

"Unlike men, she is obsessed with money." Lobster passed

another judgment on Xiao Mi.

"You don't begrudge paying."

"She doesn't want to spend a man's money. She wants to make money on her own."

"That's a good thing. Don't you like women with a job?" I felt more and more relaxed. It helped to focus on the one most important thing.

"It depends on the job, and who she does it for." We chuckled like a pair of scoundrels. He might not consider it a total loss of face for a man like me to sleep with his girl. The idea cheered me up. I gulped the last drops of whisky. My watched pointed at five-twenty in the afternoon.

XXXII

When Xiao Mi called, I felt it necessary to let her know Lobster and I were drinking in the bar. As we talked on the phone, Lobster looked around cheerfully leaning back in his chair. He also tossed a butt into the ashtray. Xiao Mi made a sound of acknowledgement. There was no way to tell her facial expression.

I passed the phone to Lobster. He said to her, "We were talking about you."

Then he chortled. After a while he looked at me while yelling into the phone, "What's the fuss about the shower! It's too early. Have something to eat first."

"Anyway you know all of us."

He laughed again at the wisecrack.

We moved to a private room in the hotel restaurant. While Lobster ordered I called Lao Xu's room. Nobody answered.

I dialed again. Someone picked it up without speaking. After some rustle Lao Xu's voice came through suddenly, "Be down in a minute!" I didn't catch the first part of his sentence. He sounded like he had just grabbed the phone.

"What's happening? Going at it again after lunch?"

"No, no—"

There was a bang over the phone and things crashed to the floor. I waited patiently. The timing was just right.

My ear pressed to the phone, I frowned at Lobster. He looked at me.

Lao Xu shouted, "Put it down!"

Then a door slammed. After a while Lao Xu spoke again, "I'm coming down."

The line went dead.

Xiao Mi called before Lao Xu's arrival to inform us that his woman had gone to her room crying. Lobster told her to bring the woman down to the restaurant. Before we hung up Lao Xu burst in panting like an old dog making his way through a fence after a three-mile dash. I pressed him into a seat before he could speak. Lobster soothed him from the other end of the table. "Take it easy. She is with Xiao Mi."

"The slut made a big scene this afternoon."

"Why?"

"A few days ago, she started talking about going to Shanghai with me."

Lobster said, "What's the big deal? Bring her back if you want to. Is Fuzhou too tough for her?"

"The slut. She took things from me." Lao Xu was still muttering incoherently. I stopped him by passing him a glass of water.

A few minutes later, Xiao Mi and the other woman came in tandem. The latter's face was smeared up with mascara. She was clutching Lao Xu's black bag with both hands. Lao Xu was so angry that he tried to slap her. Xiao Mi blocked him.

Xiao Mi tried to talk sense into her. "If you want to go to Shanghai, say it nicely. Why did you take his bag?"

The woman cried. She said Lao Xu was a liar who ate his words. Lao Xu was rendered speechless. The waiter brought some dishes in. I picked up my chopsticks urging others to eat. Nobody listened.

Lao Xu reached out for the bag. The woman half rose from her seat to protect it. Xiao Mi and I tried to persuade her in turn, but to no avail.

Lobster, who had been toasting Lao Xu, slammed the wine glass onto the table and ordered sternly, "Give it to me." The fluttered woman loosened her grip. Xiao Mi passed the bag to Lobster, who passed it to Lao Xu. Lao Xu opened it immediately to count the money inside. Then he groped for a piece of paper in the inside pocket.

The woman suddenly went mad at Lao Xu. Lao Xu dodged, stretching his arm. The woman tugged at his arm. The piece of paper was right under Lobster's nose. Piqued, Lobster seized it and unfolded it. It was the money order. I blew a smoke ring looking at him. He put it down by the wine glass. The woman, who was still tugging at Lao Xu, swung a hand backwards to keep balance. She spilled half a glass of wine on the money order. Everybody screamed. Lobster hurried to dry it with napkins. As he worked on a second napkin I saw a glint in his eyes as they were focused on the money order for a second or two.

Pushing aside chopsticks and wine glass, Lobster placed the money order between two napkins to dry it. He pressed the napkins gently without speaking. For a split second he looked at Xiao Mi, who was still trying to talk sense into the woman.

It was a dispirited meal. There was a load on everybody's mind. I started to worry. Lobster could show all cards here and now. No matter how good a card player you were, even if you were God of Gamblers, you had no chance against a robber.

However, having been his partner all these years, I knew his mantra too well: when you eat at a table with many other men, you must use your brain in order to eat more. You become a boor if you overturn the dishes. Everybody goes hungry if you overturn the table. Lobster had never been a hardliner.

Thousands of dots might have connected in Lobster's mind in the past minute. He might have solved the equation that had been snagging at him since the morning. It had taken him so long because I withheld one final clue. I had been waiting for a dramatic turn to reveal it to him, a moment when the stage was floodlit.

Other people might have overlooked the typo, especially a typo in a bright red seal impression in one's blurred memory, even if I had mentioned my doubts the other night. I had betted on Lobster's meticulousness. His eyes rolled on constant alert, catching every wisp of smoke flitting across a cavernous den. The overturned wine glass, if unintended, served the twist of plot well, like whirlpools and foams hiding running water from view. If, on the other hand, it was intended, then that woman deserved a supervisor's position in Xiao Mi's bar.

Lobster had collected himself as if he had returned from a trip into a parallel space. He spoke all of a sudden, which gave Xiao Mi such jitters that her glances at me made me believe she would beg for Lobster's mercy the next moment or point her finger at me. However, Lobster simply beckoned the waiter over to augment our order with some dim sum. The money order was dry. There was a huge water stain around the sum payable, but the specimen seal imprint was all right. Now it was back in the hands of Lao Xu, who cast quick glances at it before folding it in two and stuffing it back in the bag.

The nightclub was right on Zhongshan Road, about five to six minutes drive from the hotel. The neon light on the signboard winked at us. Two girls in cheongsam stood guarding the entrance. I suspected any light breeze would reveal the fruit patterns, apples or strawberries, whatever, on their panties. That was probably why they stood inside the glass door. Nevertheless, the fruit patterns might still peek out. We, Xiao Mi and I, stood on the curb in front of the nightclub. The five of us had to ride in two taxies. When the first taxi arrived to pick us up, Lobster had looked at the two of us with knowing eyes before laughing out, "You go first."

When our taxi made a turn, I looked back and saw them waiting for another taxi to come. I asked her, "Have you put the room key back into the drawer?"

"Yeah."

"How about the old one?"

"I tore it into pieces and flushed them down the toilet."

Neither of us talked as the taxi sped along Zhongshan

Road in the next few minutes. Changes might or might come. Who knew? The car jolted occasionally. I rolled down the car window. Strong wind rushed into the confined space. A strange idea occurred to me: are there traces of lovemaking on my bed?

"Lobster brought it into the open this afternoon in the bar."

Streetlights streamed onto her expressionless face.

"He said he knew what was going on between you and me."

I thought there was a trace of resentment in her eyes, but it might be my imagination. That Lobster had not fallen out with me despite what was going on proved he had stopped taking her seriously. She had become one of his many women.

In seven, eight or more minutes, a yellow taxi pulled up. Lobster got off from the front seat.

XXXIII

On our way back to the hotel Lao Xu was simmering with rage. His chick had clamored to go home in front of the nightclub. Lobster arranged for two other girls to keep him company. However, nobody was in high spirits. Lao Xu went up to him room alone. When the three of us came out of the elevator, Lobster swung his body and hummed a song in fake enthusiasm. In my opinion, he had overacted the whole night, especially with the two escort girls at the nightclub.

Xiao Mi stopped abruptly at the door to my room. She told him, "I'm going to sleep here tonight."

Both of us, Lobster and I, were taken aback. A smile froze on Lobster's face. The humming had stopped. His shoulders were still arched, and his hands were still in his trouser pockets. A gust of cold wind came from nowhere although we were standing in a windowless corridor. The indistinctive noise from a TV and the crying of some baby came with it.

His hands were still fidgeting with keys and coins in the pockets. His trouser legs shook slightly.

The show was disrupted. Maybe some lines had been altered in the script, or maybe a cast member simply decided to improvise. To fellow actors' embarrassment, the improvisation was too powerful to ignore. They had to react.

I had a premonition.

I waited.

Lobster never let people down. He recovered in about ten

seconds. A hand was jerked out of the trouser pocket. The arm was raised slightly, as if he was going to touch her face. In the next moment it hit her on the jaw with a thud.

I had reached out. My premonition told me that, in order to keep the show going on, I had to adapt to his improvisation. I didn't stop the raised arm in time.

I gripped Lobster by hand and dragged him into my room.

I pressed him onto the sofa. He didn't fight. Xiao Mi followed us inside.

I passed a cigarette to Lobster. We all kept a poker face.

They stared at each other. Then I heard Xiao Mi's voice. "I'm pregnant. It's his."

What a crazy scene! She might ruin a complete victory by trying to infuriate Lobster. Maybe she wanted to have her revenge before showdown. Who knew? Who could tell what was really on their minds? Anyway, she was playing with fire.

Lobster looked at me, then at her. Slowly he stood up and walked towards the door, his right hand still in the trouser pocket. When he passed her, he leaned to her ear and spoke in a soft flirty voice, "Be a good girl. Don't go too far."

Pulling open the door, he suddenly spoke to me, "Do you believe what she said?"

Ash dropped onto my pants. Before I could dust it off he had slammed the door shut.

I hurried to open the door. Instead of going into his room he was heading for the elevator. I shouted at his back in the deserted corridor, "What's the plan tomorrow?"

He waved without turning around.

"Until tomorrow."

I paused at the door for about three minutes after hearing the elevator rumble down. Then I closed it. She was squatting by the bed to get the money order out.

I sat on the sofa watching her. She unfolded the sheet of paper eagerly. After a glance she looked up at me smiling. There was a cut on her lip. It was a small cut, but enough to make her smile miserable.

She passed the piece of paper to me. As expected, there was an "o" in the specimen seal impression. In the small hours this morning, when I had pored over it, there had been an "a".

It was simple. There had been three money orders, one genuine and the other two fake. On that magic night, I swapped Lao Xu's genuine one for a fake not knowing that Xiao Mi would replace the latter with another fake a minute later. That night, I had smelled something fishy, but I couldn't put my finger on anything specific although I studied the money order over and over again.

Come to think of it, it was not the fault of mine or my brain. It was a blind spot. No player in this game had the chance to compare the genuine check with the fake side by side. Moreover, even if there had been such a chance, one might not spot the difference. The two letters looked similar. I had only caught a glimpse of the real one when Lao Cao was making it out at the bank. Later I drew what I had memorized on a sheet of paper and faxed it to Lobster. Lobster must have passed it along to the forger the same day. I had no idea who had made the mistake. It might be me or the forger.

So, the truth was that both Lao Xu and I held onto our respective fake copy without realizing that the real one had gone to Lobster. Only Lobster and Xiao Mi were in the know. That night, when I examined the fake copy, the red specimen seal impression was slightly inconsistent with my memory. What term had I used? Retinal memory? I even mentioned it to Lobster. I remembered him taking it over for a closer look. Come to think of it, there was a glint in his eyes like a wisp of smoke flitting through a cavernous den. What did he say to me then?

"It's all right. I can't tell the difference. Even if something is wrong, Lao Xu can't spot it. He won't. He will never compare them side by side."

It is true. You never know what is fake unless you compare

it with the real thing. The problem was, back then Lobster had the real thing. I believed that he must have studied the real money order that night when he went back to his room. He must have spotted the typo immediately. At that time he thought that mine was wrong, his was genuine, and the other fake copy in Lao Xu's possession must have an "a" too. He was right back then. Back then there was an "a" on the money orders Lao Xu and I had. His had an "o".

My next step was to replace Lao Xu's money order with another one carrying an "o". The two previous fake copies were identical, the nuance unrecognizable unless they were compared with the genuine one. In other words, Lobster's suspicion would be aroused if he saw an "o" on Lao Xu's money order.

In fact he had had his doubts, because out of the blue Xiao Mi was sleeping with me. For Xiao Mi, who as hard up as he was, it was safer to keep the genuine check in my place than in his hands. After all she slept in my bed. She could roll over and get it any time.

It wasn't me who had aroused his suspicion. I had stuffed the money order under the mattress in front of the two of them, which confirmed in his mind that I had nothing to do with the game of deception between Xiao Mi and him.

Therefore he wouldn't imagine my having the fourth money order made with an "o", what with the already complex scheme and the shock over finding out the thing between Xiao Mi and me. There was no way to tell whether he wanted to sound me out or he was simply befuddled when he confronted me in the bar this afternoon.

XXXIV

I didn't sleep well that night. Who could? As vehicles rumbled past the street outside, they sent flitting light across the room ceiling. From time to time, odd noises came from the night sky, the night sky that was as bluish as some icy poisonous fluid.

She fell asleep after talking to me for a while. We lay in our day clothes as if ready to leap out of the door or the window at any time. However, the truth was we had forgotten to take them off, or you could say we hadn't bothered to.

She quivered in her sleep. It might be caused by her on-and-off snoring. Her right cheek was buried in the pillow. The corners of her mouth went awry, which made the cut on her lip more conspicuous. The cut moved up and down in beat with her breathing, as if offering me an explanation. Her breath wasn't pleasant. It was an acrid sour smell.

Now the money order was in Xiao Mi's purse between our tangled bodies. The greater part of it was under her waist, but I could still feel it against my groin. I ignored the discomfort.

Money is nothing to me. I mean, money is just part of a game. There are two kinds of money in the world, one to keep people alive and the other to play a game. The latter has nothing to do with most people. The few that actually play the game don't see the difference when they start.

Once they are in the game they find that money simply flows in a small cycle. Nobody knows where it comes from; neither can anyone claim it as his own and end the game. The cycle goes on and on. Players in the game make a fuss about it on the gambling table. A rod pushes the money hither and wither. When the money is piled in front of a gambler, he is ecstatic. Once the money is pushed away to another player, the thought of winning it back makes him even more ecstatic.

God divides money into two piles, one for guys who know their place and the other for those who don't. He makes the latter play an unending game to deplete their energy. This must be the biggest fraud in the world. However, the game is so enticing that, even if you have seen it through, you can't help playing.

I fell asleep around dawn and woke up when Xiao Mi left the bed. We had a tight schedule today. Upon leaving I saw myself in the mirror, a haggard face with tired eyes.

We rode the elevator down to the restaurant. Around a quarter to nine we walked out of the restaurant and rode the elevator up. Instead of getting into our room we went to the other end of the corridor, used the fire exit to reach the fourth floor, crossed the deserted western-style restaurant and walked into the attached kitchen. Nobody was around. There was a door on the other end of the kitchen. It opened to an elevator for hotel staff. Out of the elevator on the ground level was a tiled passageway leading to the hotel docking bay. A truck was being unloaded. Nobody paid us attention.

We hailed a taxi from there.

I handed the money order to the bank teller. She had arrived for work a few minutes before. With a newly made cup of tea she had sat at the corporate banking counter waiting for the first customer of the day. I had also presented two ID cards, mine and that of Lao Xu's. Lao Xu was most probably still sleeping. He had not checked his black bag. If he had, he would find an ID with the picture of a man neither he nor I knew. I asked Xiao Mi to buy a fake ID card from the street yesterday. Any ID, as long as it was a man's, I had told her.

It being a Monday, the teller slouched a bit after a day off.

In twenty minutes the one million yuan was transferred to Xiao Mi's account. I pocketed the seal. It was five minutes to ten. There were two plane tickets in Xiao Mi's purse. The plane was to leave for Shanghai at five minutes past eleven.

We hurried out of the bank. As we passed the door, I looked back at the electronic clock on the bank wall because I never trusted my own watch. Lobster came into view. There were a row of couches by the glass wall along the street. Instead of sitting on any of them Lobster was standing. The morning sun penetrated the maroon glass onto his right cheek. His left cheek remained in the shadow. It was hard to say whether he was smiling or not.

I froze, opening my mouth as if to address him out of reflex. Xiao Mi turned around abruptly. In seconds she saw everything. I grabbed her by the arm and we rushed out. Lobster seemed to be speaking to two guys near him.

There was no taxi available. We ran frantically along the curb. Pedestrians parted to make way for us. At the turn I looked back. Lobster was standing by a grey Santana at the bank entrance. His right hand yanked the car door open, his left hand pointing at us. He seemed to be yelling.

After the turn was a narrow lane of about fifty meters. At the other end of it was a broad road. Xiao Mi ran ahead of me. I was dumbfounded. How could it be possible for Lobster to show up at the bank? He should be at the hotel, at least this morning. He should first get hold of Lao Xu's ID card.

About ten meters into the lane, I heard tires screech to a stop. The grey Santana was parked at the head of the lane. All four doors were thrown open. People jumped out. I ran faster.

I took the seal out of my pocket and squeezed it into Xiao Mi's hand. As we were about to run out of the alley a motorcycle roared towards us. I stopped. Xiao Mi had sprinted out of the lane waving at a vacant taxi. I shouted at her, "Go, go, go!"

I turned around. Lobster was about twenty meters away. Behind him ran a couple of figures. It was the fat guy and the thin guy again. Since they were running at high speed the contrast was not as comical as before. I realized that Lobster was not on his feet until too late. He was riding a crimson motorcycle. A sharp pain penetrated my eardrum. An enormous force ripped my groin like a red blitz. However, the force ebbed into a gentle rubbing in half a second.

When I came to, I was lying on the ground, my occipital bone against a bump on the wall. Lobster leaned his face towards my abdomen murmuring something. Sunlight shone from the eaves about ten meters away, creating a red glow along his auricle. There was one more thing to do. I cursed my slow brain.

The realization made me hasten to reach for my phone. The inside of my trouser pocket felt sticky. I took out the phone, pressed several digits, and waited. It was such a long wait, longer than the first half of my life. Without thinking, my hand dodged Lobster's foot. Lao Cao's voice came from the other end of the phone. I couldn't hold the phone higher. It was about fifty centimeters above my chin. I shouted into the phone, "Don't worry. I'll explain."

XXXV

Another night. Music. The clinking of glasses. My mind wandered back to Lü Yan.

"Things are not what they were. Nobody leaves money around. Everyone keeps money in a locked drawer and hang the key on the belt," Lü Yan blabbered. He had drunk too much.

"It's a good thing," he continued. "We should have laid down the rules earlier. We can't share money among each other. We should keep money in our own drawer, together with an account book. I told you before. Money is different from women. Didn't I?"

He laughed in a weird voice, as if the sound had squeezed out of his throat, forced through the uvula, rolled several times between the velum and the root of tongue. You might believe he was clearing his throat, or imagine a cassette got caught in the cassette player.

"Very smart," he said. "Three cards. You kicked some ass."

I had never told him anything about it. However, stories circulated in our circle. By and by they became legends. At the moment our story was hot, because, reportedly, I had caused Lobster a loss of one million yuan with a street hoax.

"You have to tell me about it another time," Lü Yan continued. "Have you played bluffing? It is a clever game, not as clever as yours, but quite clever. Have you played such a card game? You lay three cards on their faces and tell the next player they are three queens. He can pretend to believe you and put three kings on top of them. When you flip the cards over and they are not queens, you have to take the cards back. However, if they're indeed three queens, he has to take the cards back. It all hinges on him. His other alternative is to uphold the bluffing and pass the buck to the next player, who then has to decide whether to flip the cards or not. Anyone who decides to flip runs the risk of taking in all the cards and losing the game. That is the key. Who doesn't want to keep bluffing? There is the extra advantage of getting rid of cards you don't want. Everybody knows everybody is bluffing, but no one wants to take responsibility and face consequences. That's the key."

Another woman sat beside him, not Sisi. I didn't know her name, but names were not important to them anyway. We were in a bar on Yan'an Road near Urumuqi Road. It was a prime location for a bar because there were many other bars and hotels around. At night, you could smell out people like you among passers-by outside. Upon first sniff it was a smell of indolence, but then, if they were truly comrades, you would recognize the hormone of tension, a frequent smell on gambling tables.

Xiao Mi was the nominal proprietor of the bar. However, she had only one third of stakes. One third of the monthly profit went to Lao Cao. Another one third was mine. There were two stories in the bar. In the private rooms on the upper floor, guests were entertained by escort girls dispatched by a madam from Fujian Province.

It was ten at night. I sat at the lobby downstairs among night animals. The karaoke was on. The DJ sat idle in his little booth by the bar counter because no one felt like singing at the moment. Some actors and actresses from Hong Kong were singing and dancing on the huge rear projection screen. The dim lights above their head were rendered dimmer by the screen. They frolicked about two centimeters above my eyes like some ghosts. I suspected that the French painter named Henri de Toulouse-Lautrec, who made whores in his paintings drift in ballrooms and bars like ghosts, had always observed real whores from below, because he was a midget.

Lü Yan rose to take his girl to bed. We no longer lived together. A year ago, after I had been discharged from the hospital, we gave up the apartment on Yandang Road. Since then I had been sitting in this bar every night. She might be in or not. If she was out, she would come back at around eleven, so that we could go home together.

I'm living with Xiao Mi in a place we rented together on Zhenning Road near Urumuqi Road.

I drank slowly, one glass at a time. It was always Chivas Regal Year Twelve. I had been so accustomed to it that I felt like it was the milk I drank upon birth. Tonight, she stayed out longer than usual.

Earlier tonight a gang of us had dinner at Café de Coral. Xiao Mi was there too. A guy suddenly asked, "Lobster hasn't been around. Where is he?"

He was a minor figure. I had seen him two or three times before when we had dinner parties every night, when people we did and didn't know, people we thought we knew but actually we didn't, and people we thought we didn't know but actually we did, ate and drank together. We seemed to have dropped such a habit. Or maybe I had stopped going.

The conversation concentrated on Lobster for a while. One guy reported seeing him in Sanya while another claimed to have bumped into him in Xinjiang. I didn't know his whereabouts, though most likely he was trying new ways of making money. He was always trying as long as trouble didn't catch up with him. Even if he got into trouble, he would get over it and start trying again. One day he would be really rich. One day he would be led out of the gambling floor where everybody played and shown into a private room for rich people only.

But who knows? Maybe all his efforts will come to nothing. Maybe Lao Cao will become filthily rich one day. It is a different age where guys like Lao Cao prevail. The problem with Lobster, or with me, is that we're single-minded. The two of us were born in the wrong era. We set our goal and go at it without looking sideways. We regard the world as a card game under our control, but the real world always surprises us.

Halfway through the dinner Xiao Mi answered a phone call. A few minutes later she left.

She came into the bar around midnight. After casting a glance my direction, she went first to the cash register, then upstairs. In about ten minutes, she came down. I stood up without waiting for her to come over. I summoned a taxi for both of us to go home.

We didn't talk in the taxi. It was always the case if she came back to the bar late. Every time she came back late, she leaned languidly against me closing her eyes, as if she was too tired to hold herself up. Light chased shadows inside the taxi. She had a soft complexion. I didn't kiss her. Maybe she wanted a kiss, or maybe not.

I rolled down the window a bit to let the night wind wash off the indistinct smell. Some other man's smell lingered on her, or maybe it was my imagination. The smell started about half a year ago. Neither her shampoo nor her menthol cigarettes could cover up that smell of dissolution.

I hadn't asked her. She volunteered the information. I had seen the guy. He had a pale face with a wisp of hair in his eye. He flaunted his ass the way a young male dog stuck up its tail. I had probably seen him standing outside the glass door of Café de Coral. Who cares!

She said, "It doesn't matter. He doesn't matter. He's just a man."

He was just a boy.

"You two are not the same. We just meet for a drink or two. Spur of the moment."

Drink as much as you want. It didn't matter indeed. But I detested the smell of their drinks. I bought myself a bottle of Davidoff perfume. If you regard the blue bottle in the light, you can picture a naked woman squatting and wriggling in some icy poisonous fluid.

We lived in peace with each other, really. Just the two of us. There were only two people living in our place. A third had almost arrived, but again it might be an illusion. Back in the hospital I had suggested abortion, although there might be no baby at all, because from my angle on the sickbed, her belly looked no different from usual. Beneath the black-and-white floral patterned blouse, her belly was as flat and soft as usual. I made the suggestion to her. No, I believed the baby was mine. I remembered how I had tried frantically to fish out that shoddy condom between her curled legs.

She collapsed onto me. Actually she was lying on my lap. She opened her eyes to look at me. Her hand touched my mouth. Although I didn't feel like it, I kissed her eventually. Her mouth felt like a dissolving mint.

The taxi stopped. I paid. We went upstairs. The door was opened and then closed. She didn't turn on the light. Neither did I reach out for the Clipsal switch by the door. We looked at each other in darkness, our eyes glittering like those of nocturnal animals. She caressed my face, her hand as cold as the claw of a kitten that had just climbed down a water pipe.

The curtain was drawn back. The window was half shut. The gauze curtain swung in the breeze. The night was tender. I sat on the bed kissing her and caressing her until her body steamed up like meat fresh out of an oven. I pressed my face against her temple. There was the smell of shampoo in her hair, plus some other smell that never went away.

I didn't undress her, but her hand went to my belt and then the zipper.

She took my thing out. Now it was in the moonlight between her and me. It hung loosely like a used condom. She lowered her head to put it into her mouth.

Lobster had taken his revenge. According to the doctors, the motorcycle ruined a part of me.

Stories by Contemporary Writers from Shanghai